P9-BYY-425

THE HIDDEN CORONET

CATHERINE FISHER

THE HIDDEN CORONET

Dial Books
an imprint of Penguin Group (USA) Inc.

DIAL BOOKS
An imprint of Penguin Group (USA) Inc.
Published by The Penguin Group
Penguin Group (USA) Inc., 375 Hudson Street, New York, NY 10014, U.S.A.

Penguin Group (Canada), 90 Eglinton Avenue East, Suite 700, Toronto, Ontario, Canada M4P 2Y3 (a division of Pearson Penguin Canada Inc.) • Penguin Books Ltd, 80 Strand, London WC2R 0RL, England • Penguin Ireland, 25 St. Stephen's Green, Dublin 2, Ireland (a division of Penguin Books Ltd) • Penguin Group (Australia), 250 Camberwell Road, Camberwell, Victoria 3124, Australia (a division of Pearson Australia Group Pty Ltd) • Penguin Books India Pvt Ltd, 11 Community Centre, Panchsheel Park, New Delhi - 110 017, India • Penguin Group (NZ), 67 Apollo Drive, Rosedale, Auckland 0632, New Zealand (a division of Pearson New Zealand Ltd) • Penguin Books (South Africa) (Pty) Ltd, 24 Sturdee Avenue, Rosebank, Johannesburg 2196, South Africa • Penguin Books Ltd, Registered Offices: 80 Strand, London WC2R 0RL, England

First published in the United States 2011
by Dial Books
an imprint of Penguin Group (USA) Inc.

First published in Great Britain by The Bodley Head Children's Books 2000
Copyright © 2000 by Catherine Fisher
All rights reserved
The publisher does not have any control over and does not assume any responsibility for author or third-party websites or their content.

Designed by Nancy R. Leo-Kelly
Text set in Sabon
Printed in the U. S. A.
1 3 5 7 9 10 8 6 4 2

Library of Congress Cataloging-in-Publication Data
Fisher, Catherine, date.
The hidden Coronet / by Catherine Fisher.
p. cm. — (Relic Master ; 3)
Summary: Sixteen-year-old Raffi and Master Galen continue to evade the Watch as they seek the Coronet, a potent ancient relic that could be their only hope for defeating the power that is destroying Anara.
ISBN 978-0-8037-3675-7 (hardcover)
[1. Fantasy. 2. Apprentices—Fiction. 3. Antiquities—Fiction.] I.Title.
PZ7.F4995Hid 2011 [Fic]—dc22 2010039315

To Colin

Contents

THE HIDDEN CORONET

Frost Fair

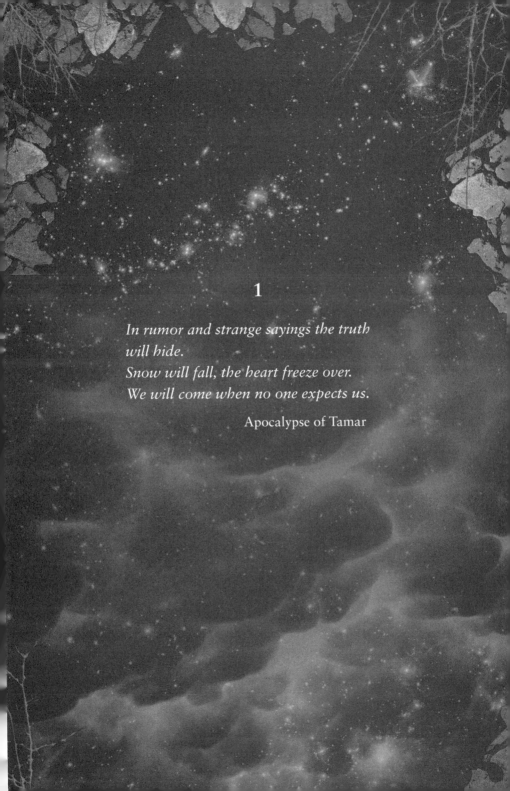

1

*In rumor and strange sayings the truth
will hide.
Snow will fall, the heart freeze over.
We will come when no one expects us.*

Apocalypse of Tamar

TWO MEN SAT ON A BENCH ON THE ICE.

Between them a brazier glowed with hot coals, its metal feet sinking into a pool of meltwater.

They sat silent, in the heart of the Frost Fair; in its racket of bleating sheep, barking dogs, innumerable traders calling their wares and, above all, the ominous hammering. Meats sizzled on spits, babies screamed, jugglers threw jingling bells, fiddlers played for coins, and in cushioned booths Sekoi of all colors told spellbinding stories, their voices unnaturally sharp and ringing in the bitter cold.

Finally the older man stirred. "Are you sure?" he muttered.

"I heard it in Tarkos. Then again last week in Lari-minier Market. It's certain." The cobbler, still in his leather apron, stared bleakly out at the black Watchtower in the center of the frozen lake, as if afraid its sentinels could hear him from there.

"He's been seen?"

"So they say." The cobbler's dirty heel scratched at a fish skeleton frozen in the ice; its wide eye stared up at him. "There's been a lot of talk. Prophecies and odd rumors. What I heard was, that on Flainsnight last year there was an enormous explosion. The House of Trees split wide and out of it, on black wings, a vision rose up into the sky, huge over Tasceron." He glanced around, making the sign of honor furtively with his hand. "It was him. The Crow."

The old man spat. "Incredible! What did it look like?"

"Huge. Black. A bird and not a bird. You know, like it said in the old Book."

"I might. And it spoke?"

"So the woman who told me said."

A scar-bull clattered by pulled by two men, its hooves

slipping on the glassy lake. When they had gone the old man shrugged. "Could be just rumor."

The cobbler glanced around, worried. Behind them a peddler was hawking ribbons and pins and fancy lace, a crowd was watching two men come to blows over the price of geese, and a boy was turning cartwheels among the stalls, a few coppers in his cap on the ice. The cobbler drew up closer and dropped his voice. "No. Why do you think the Watch have doubled their patrols? They've heard; they have spies everywhere."

"So what did it say, this vision?"

"It said, '*Listen Anara, your Makers are coming back to you; through the darkness and emptiness I call them. Flain and Tamar and Soren, even Kest will come. They will dispel the darkness. They will scatter the power of the Watch.*'"

The words, barely whispered, seemed dangerous, charged with power, as if they sparked in the freezing air. In the silence that followed, the racket of the fair seemed louder; both men were glad of it. The peddler had spilled his tray and was kneeling on the ice, picking up pins awkwardly with numb fingers. The wind scuttered a few closer to the brazier, like silver slivers.

The old man held gloved hands to the heat. "Well, if it's true . . ."

"It is."

". . . Then it will change the world. I pray I live to see it." He looked ruefully over the tents and stalls to the Watchtower, glinting with frost. "But unless the Makers come tomorrow, it'll be too late for those poor souls."

From here the hammering was louder. The half-constructed gallows were black, a rickety structure of high timbers built directly onto the ice, one man up there now on a ladder, hauling up the deadly swinging nooses of rope. Above him the sky was iron-gray, full of unfallen sleet. Smoke from the fair's fires rose into it, a hundred straight columns.

"Another black frost tonight," the cobbler muttered.

The old man didn't answer. Instead, he said, "I hear one of the prisoners is a keeper."

The cobbler almost sat upright. Then he relapsed onto the rough bench, biting his thumbnail. "Dear God," he whispered. "To hang?"

"To hang. Tomorrow, like all the rest."

Frost Fair

Over the lake the hammering ended abruptly. The nooses swung, empty, frost already glinting on them.

The peddler picked up the last needle. He straightened with a groan, then limped over. "Goods, gentlemen?" he whined. "Samples of ribbon. Beads. Bright scarves. Something for the wife?"

The cobbler shook his head sourly; the old man smiled. "Dead, my friend. Long dead."

"Ah, well." The peddler was gray-haired; he eased the crutch wearily under his arm. "Not even a brooch to put on your coat?"

"Nothing. Not today."

Indifferently, as if he was used to it, the peddler shrugged. "It's a raw day to walk down a long road," he said quietly.

They looked at him, bemused.

"Fellow's drunk," the cobbler muttered.

THE PEDDLER HOBBLED AWAY between tents and around a pen of bleating sheep, their small hooves scratching the frozen lake, down to the stall of a pastry-seller, where he bought a hot pie and ate half of it, crouched by the heat of an open oven. Grease scorched his fingers through the torn gloves. He bent forward, his long gray hair swinging out of his hood, but as he pulled himself slightly upright on the crutch a close watcher might have glimpsed, just for an instant, that he was a tall man, and not as old or as crippled as he seemed.

Someone squeezed in beside him. "Is that for me?"

The peddler handed over the remains of the pie without comment; the boy who had been cartwheeling wolfed it down ravenously, barely stopping for breath.

The peddler's eyes watched the crowd intently.

"Well?"

"Nothing. I tried the password on a woman and she told me to get lost or she'd call the Watch." Raffi licked every flake of pastry from his fingers, still uneasy at the memory. "You?"

"Not our contact, no. But I overheard an interesting conversation."

"What about?"

"A certain black bird."

Raffi stared up, alarmed. "Again?" He rubbed his

Frost Fair

greasy hands nervously on his jerkin, then almost as a reflex unfurled a sense-line and sent it out, but the noisy crowd made him giddy with all their sensations and arguments and chatter; and under them was only the impenetrable glass-blue barrier of the ice, the vast lake frozen to its depths, the tiny creatures down there sluggish, only half alive.

"Rumors are spreading," Galen said grimly. "Perhaps we have Alberic to thank. His people could never keep secrets." He glanced around. "Though such stories may be useful. They'll make people think. Stir their faith."

Raffi rubbed his cold arms, frowning as the oven door was slammed shut. Then he smiled. "What would they say if they knew the Crow was right here?"

Galen's rebuke struck him behind his eyes—a mind-flare—so that he winced. The keeper stepped closer, his gaunt face hard. "Will you keep your mouth shut! Don't talk to me unless you have to. And stay close!"

He turned, pushing through the crowd. Eyes wet, furious, Raffi glared after him.

They were both so tense they could barely talk anymore. They had been at the fair since yesterday. Every hour they spent here was a sickening danger; there were Watchmen everywhere, and Raffi had been searched once already at a checkpoint. That still made his skin crawl. But Galen wouldn't go until the contact came. And they had no idea who it would be.

All afternoon he tried to keep warm. The cold was numbing. The stalls and awnings were brittle with ice; long, jagged spikes of it that dripped for a few hours at midday and then hardened again in the terrible nights, so that the whole fair was encased in a glassy splendor, like the Castle of Halen must once have been.

Despite himself, Raffi thought of Sarres. The hall would be warm there; the Sekoi would be telling some story, with the little girl, Felnia, curled up on its lap and Tallis, the Guardian of the place, stoking the fire with logs. And Carys. What would she be doing? He wanted to be back there so much that it hurt.

Earlier, someone had thrown a few coppers to him; now to ease his depression he spent it on a small slab of sticky toffee. Twisting off a corner he sucked it with delight, trying not to chew, to make the incredible sweetness last. It had been years since he'd tasted anything like it. Five years. Since he'd left home. He saw Galen watching him darkly across a pen of sheep, but he didn't care. Someone jogged his elbow, almost shoving him into the pen.

"Sorry," the woman said.

"It's all right." Raffi pocketed the toffee before he dropped it.

She smiled at him. "Cold makes me clumsy. And it's a raw day to walk down a long road."

He froze, swallowing the whole lump without tasting it. He glanced at her sidelong; a big farm woman, fair hair scraped back, a bold, red face. For a moment he had no idea what to do; then he sent a sense-line snaking over to Galen, saw the peddler's head turn instantly, his hasty limping through the crowd.

Raffi took a breath. "Not if there's a warm welcome at the end of it," he managed.

Relief flickered in the woman's eyes, brief but unmistakable. "Is he here?" she muttered.

Raffi caught her arm. "Beads?" he said in a normal voice. "Here's your man."

He dragged her over to Galen. Their eyes met; she

picked up objects from the tray at random, examining them.

"Thank God," she whispered. "I thought I'd never find you! We have to get home now, while the place is empty."

Galen glanced around; Raffi knew he was wary of a trap.

"How far?"

"Three miles. Over the hill. I have a cart outside the west checkpoint."

"Then we go separately. Different exits. Meet outside."

The woman nodded. She looked resolute.

"What's your name?" Galen asked quietly.

"Caxton, Majella Caxton. You will come?"

"Have faith, woman. We won't fail you."

Dumping the lace, she strode away. Galen watched her, then said, "Go ahead of me. No contact, whatever happens."

THERE WAS A LINE AT THE CHECKPOINT. All the entrances to the fair were thronged, because the Watch took a third of all profits, or more if they disliked your face, and everyone had to be checked in and out.

Raffi folded back his sleeve. This was the worst part. Despite the cold, he was sweating.

"Next!"

He crossed to the table and showed the number painted on his wrist. The Watchman perched there flicked through his list. Glancing back, Raffi saw Galen among a group of men carrying wool-bales.

"Canver. Michael?"

He nodded.

"Performer. Ha, I know what that means. Pickpocket. Beggar."

"No!" Terrified, Raffi looked up. "I tumble, juggle."

"With what?"

"Apples."

"So where are they?"

He shrugged. "I ate them."

"You must think I was born yesterday." The Watchman was young, with a cruel, thin mouth. "Turn out your pockets," he said.

Raffi hadn't expected this. After all, he had no profits. But if they even suspected he was a thief he would lose a hand, and the thought of that made him turn cold.

He dumped two small coins and the toffee.

"Is that it?" The Watchman grinned. "Come here."

The search was quick, but thorough. It left him hot with fear and embarrassment, and it found nothing. The Watchman's snort was derisory. "Hardly worth your coming, was it?" He scooped up the toffee and shoved it into his own pocket. "Now get lost."

Trembling with anger and relief, Raffi turned.

He had only taken two steps when the man said, "Wait."

Raffi stopped. His heart thudded like a hammerbird. Slowly he turned; the Watchman smiled coldly, arrogant on the slippery ice. He had a different list in his hand. Glancing down at it again he muttered, "Come back here."

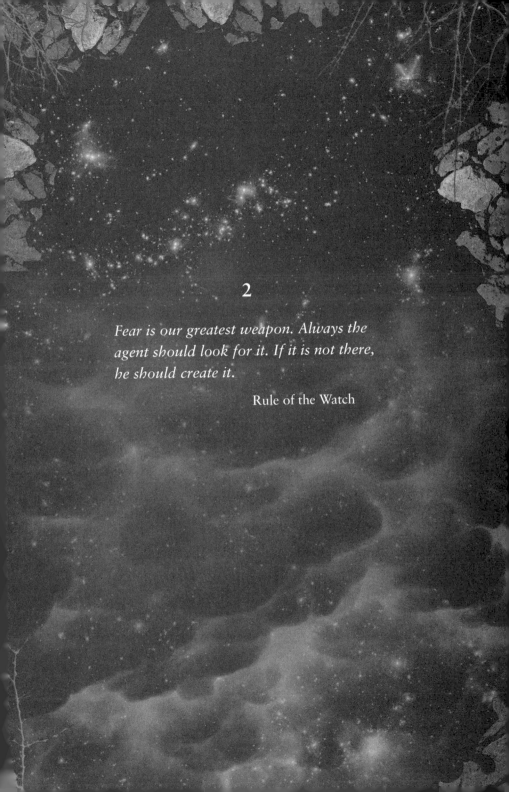

2

Fear is our greatest weapon. Always the agent should look for it. If it is not there, he should create it.

Rule of the Watch

E

VERYTHING SEEMED TO GO QUIET.

Raffi barely breathed; his whole body was a rigidity of terror, so that for an instant there was nothing else in the world.

Then, as if from a long distance, he heard Galen at the other table, grumbling to the harassed Watchman there about the cold, and even the sound of his voice brought Raffi a sliver of courage.

He walked back. "What?" he muttered, his voice shaky.

The Watchman thrust the paper in his hands. "Look at

that," he said in a bored voice. "Have you seen any of them?"

Raffi turned it around.

It was a list of outlaws. Each one was pictured—a brief sketch—and underneath their names, a sum of money for their capture, a list of crimes. He looked at it quickly, then gave it back.

"I can't read," he lied.

"You can see, can't you! Do you know any of them?"

"No."

The man leered, his breath smelling of sour beer. "Well, keep your eyes open, bright boy. It'll pay you more than juggling apples."

Hurrying away, Raffi bit his lip.

Carys's name had been on the list.

The drawing of her had been incredibly accurate; her sharp look, the short, straight brown hair. Underneath it had said:

CARYS ARRIN. FORMER WATCHSPY. INS. 547 SILVER. MARN MOUNTAIN.

WANTED ALIVE FOR ABDUCTION, TREASON, COUNTERESPIONAGE.

A PRIORITY TARGET.

30,000 MARKS.

Frost Fair

It was a fortune! But then, it would be. She'd betrayed the Watch, kidnapped one of their children, walked out on Braylwin. They'd hunt her down till they found her.

He stumbled, barely noticing, thanking God and the Makers that she was safe back on Sarres. She'd wanted to come with them, but Galen had refused absolutely, ignoring her anger. She was like Galen. Though they both loved Sarres, they grew restless there.

"Boy!"

The big woman was waiting on the cart, her sacking sleeves rolled past her elbows. Brawny arms controlled the fidgeting marset in the harness.

Raffi climbed up beside her.

"Where's your master?"

"Behind," he said wearily.

She looked at him shrewdly. "You got through, didn't you? Must be a tough life though."

He rubbed his hair with his hands, silent, annoyed she could see he was scared, annoyed with himself.

They watched the gate. When Galen came through it he hobbled away up the road ahead of them, ignoring them. The woman whipped up the reins and the marset stumbled off, Raffi grabbing tight. They soon passed the keeper. On the ice the cart ran smooth, but when the wheels hit the rough track the lurching began, a giddy swaying up the treeless slopes, down splintering ruts. The road was bleak, all its vegetation seared to blackness by the relentless frosts, except that halfway up, a small, bent patch of bramble thicket clung on. The woman stopped the cart there, and they waited for Galen.

He walked easier now, the limp reduced to normal, and when he came up he dumped the peddler's tray and the pack with relief among the wool-bales, brushing ash-paste out of his hair in disgust.

Then he looked up at her.

"You must be in sore need of a keeper, Majella Caxton."

"I am, master. Believe me." She said it calmly, her shrewd gray eyes on his. "Or I'd never have run the risk. Yours or mine."

For a moment he studied her. Then, as if a question had been answered, he nodded and climbed into the back, stretching his legs out among the wool-bales. "Is it a relic?"

"God knows." She started the marset moving. "It terrifies the beasts, fills me with dark horrors I wouldn't try to describe. We're haunted by something, master. We can't even live in the house anymore. And if you don't get rid of it, it will surely kill someone."

Galen didn't answer, though Raffi knew he was intrigued. But the woman was busy now with the driving; ice made the rough track treacherous. Twice the marset slipped, its hooves clattering, and she had to urge it on. "Come on, my darling," she crooned. "Up you go."

Turning, Raffi saw the Frost Fair already far below them, a squalor of stalls and pens and smoke darkening the pure lake, and beyond it at the northern shore the quenta forest, dark and ominous, its strange tangled trees forming impenetrable thickets.

He also saw the gallows.

Galen was looking at them too. The keeper's black eyes were angry and thoughtful; as Raffi watched he fished among the trinkets of the peddler's tray and brought out the awen-beads, jet and green, slipping them on over his head. He held out Raffi's and Raffi took them, the two blue and purple strands of the scholar, wishing Galen would say something about the gallows. When he was silent he was planning, and Raffi feared that.

Slowly, the cart rocked to the top of the hill. ·

The way down was less steep; the woman took a breath and said, "Now. You want to hear all about it."

"It would help."

She glanced over her shoulder at him as he leaned among the soft bales.

"Well, we moved here two months ago. We're Watch-tenants. We had a farm up north, but then out of the blue they moved us. No explanations. When I saw this place I was amazed. It's old, you'll see that. Far too good for me and a dozen farm men. Lots of the rooms are empty."

"What's it called?" Galen interrupted.

"Halenden." She flicked the reins. "For a fortnight it was all right. Then the trouble started."

"Noises?"

She shrugged, uneasy. "Hideous sounds. First time it brought us all hurtling out of our beds. I thought some beggar-band was burning the place around our ears.

Frost Fair

Howling, echoing deep down. Max—the foreman—swears it's some Kest-ghost, trapped under the place. He's a loudmouth, and I'd sack him, but I need him. Most of the others have left."

The cart jolted; Raffi clung on, feeling sick.

"What else?" Galen murmured.

"Things move. Around the place. They're never where you left them. Doors won't open; then they open on their own. Plates smash. Voices talk in rooms where no one is. But last week, that was the worst."

She stopped the cart suddenly and turned to face him, her broad face red with the cold. "I'm not a woman who scares easily, master."

"I can see that," he said.

"Then you'll know that I'm scared now." The wind gusted sleet in her eyes; she rubbed it away. "Last week, on Agramonsday, I was alone in the house. The men were in the fields. I was sure I heard something moving down below. There's a cellar, a deep cellar. It sounded like . . ." She shook her head, impatient with herself. "Flain knows what. I'm not good with words. A dragging sound. Cold. Heavy."

The wind was icy. Raffi shivered, tugging his hands up into his sleeves. In all the bleak land around him nothing stirred, the hedges gnawed down to bare thorn.

"You went down?" Galen asked, his face intent.

"I did."

"Not many would have."

"Keeper, I don't like mysteries. I'm a plain woman; I trust what my senses tell me. I took a lamp and went down the cellar steps." She paused. Raffi felt a threat of terror break out in her, the shock of it stirring the small hairs on the backs of his hands.

Then she said, "I saw it. A shadow. Something evil. A terrible . . . venom seemed to come from it. I knew it was alive."

The marset whinnied, impatient. Sleet was coming down heavily now, a white sheet of weather slanting out of the west.

Galen didn't move.

The woman turned back to the harness. "That's all I can tell you. It vanished. I was outside, shivering, when the men came back; can't even remember how I got there. None of us will stay in the place now—we've fitted up a

Frost Fair

barn a few fields off and even the dogs creep in with us at night."

The cart's wheels began to turn, crunching down into the ruts and up again. "Can you help us?" she asked quietly.

Galen leaned back. "Is there anything else you want to tell me?"

"No," she said, too quickly.

He gazed at her broad back. Then he said, "I can only do what the Makers wish."

For the rest of the journey he was silent, and glancing back Raffi knew he was meditating, gathering strength, sending sense-lines out into the frozen land, waking stones and soil and the bare trees, searching for any Maker-life, any energies.

Raffi was quiet too. After the strain and racket of the fair, weariness washed over him like a wave. Despite the cold he dozed, slumping against the woman. As the cart hit a stone he jolted awake, muttering, "Sorry." She grinned at him. "My lad was like you once. Eat and sleep. That's all boys are good for."

He smiled, wan.

The evening closed in. Above in the darkening sky the seven moons brightened, the crescent of Cyrax far off on the horizon; glinting through torn cloud above the black land. Stars were suddenly there too, vast scatterings of light, brilliant in the frost-cold.

The road ran down, into a hollow. Raffi felt trees, dark shapes on each side, old hollies and some yew, the faint turpy smell of their needles crushed under the wheels.

The track ran smoother. The trees closed in, became a dim avenue, their branches tangling overhead. Bats flitted in a narrow strip of sky.

And then he felt the house.

His eyes widened; the skin crawled on his neck. Behind him, he heard Galen scramble up.

Halenden was dark; a cluster of roofs and gables rising above the trees. He could see windows, most of them boarded up, and a great mass of ivy and spidervine that sprawled over half the façade, smothering walls and chimneys.

As they drove up to it, the house seemed to grow. Owls called in its leaves; a skeat answered in the woods, and then a whole pack of them was howling, the farm dogs barking furiously in return.

The cart creaked to a halt.

Galen climbed out, stiff, then stood tall in his dark coat, looking up at the building, noting the battered, rain-stained door, the high windows, some with broken glass, glittering with reflections of the climbing moons.

The dogs went quiet with a yelp, as if he'd ordered them to.

Raffi stood behind him. The stillness of the place made him wary. The woods were infected by its gloom; the house had eyes inside, and for a second he looked through them, seeing himself and Galen and Majella from some high place.

"Come around the back," the woman said, climbing down awkwardly.

But when Galen turned, her face went suddenly still because there was something changed about him, some power that crackled in the air; his face was gaunt and his eyes dark in the shadows.

"I know," he said.

Barely breathing she mumbled, "Keeper?"

He stepped toward her. Now he was the Crow, the dark energies moving in blue sparks through his fingers. "I know. The Makers have told me. The very trees have told me. Do you believe you could really hide this from me?"

The woman gasped. For a moment Raffi thought she would kneel down in the mud, her fingers making the half-forgotten signs of honor. But then she looked up boldly, her face set.

"You're right. I should have told you."

"Told us what?" Raffi blurted out. He couldn't bear it. "Is this a trap? Are the Watch here?"

Galen grinned sourly. "In a manner of speaking. What she hasn't told us is that this is the house of a Watchman. Her son's house. Isn't that so?"

She nodded bleakly.

Raffi was aghast. "We've got to get out!"

To his horror Galen just laughed. "Oh, I don't think so. I don't think he even knows."

"He doesn't." She looked up at him, her small eyes measuring his anger. "He'd have us all killed if he found out."

Frost Fair

"Your own son!" Raffi couldn't believe it.

"My own son." Watching Galen she said, "The keeper knows. He knows we don't stop loving our children, however they turn out. Yes, my son is a Watchman. He wasn't taken as a child; he joined them of his own will. He enjoys power. He hates the Order. You've even seen him, lad. He was the one who searched you back at the checkpoint."

Raffi's chest was tight with fear. "We have to go. He'll recognize me!"

But Galen was watching the woman, his face unreadable. Finally he asked, "Will he come here?"

"Unlikely. Not while the fair is on. He'll want to see the hangings."

Galen nodded. "Then listen to me. Tonight, if I can, I will break your house of its spell. But in return, if I survive, I want your help. Your son has a spare uniform, insignia, papers. I want them."

"What!" Raffi grasped the keeper's arm. "Why?"

Galen shook him off ferociously. "Because if we do nothing, there are ten people who'll hang on those gallows. And one of them is a keeper. I intend to get him out."

Chilled, Raffi stared at him in despair.

And instantly, from behind them in the house, an eerie, throaty cry rose up, as if it were his own fear given voice, an echoing howl from some creature trapped in unendurable darkness and pain, so terrifying that Raffi's hands went cold and all his sense-lines stirred in a web of dizzying sickness.

It lasted long seconds. When it had ebbed, all three of them were still, shadows among shadows.

Then the woman nodded, white-faced.

"All right," she said. "Anything."

3

One day Soren was walking in the Fields of Eldaman when she saw a tiny flower under her foot. "What are you called?" she asked. The flower said it had no name. Soren picked it and wove it into a crown. She took it to Flain. "In our work," she said, "we have overlooked the least and smallest of lives."

Flain ran his fingers over the flowers. "From now on," he said, "all men will know you. You will teach the highest how to be humble."

Book of the Seven Moons

THE ROOM WAS VERY DARK. Galen would have only one lamp, and that was standing in the middle of the floor. Its yellow glow threw a great shadow over the keeper's shoulder, edging his face with slants of light. Around it he was arranging the awen-beads, seven circles of green and jet, a peculiar formation new to Raffi.

Squeezed into the corner, his back against the dusty paneling, Raffi sat hugging his knees, then laid his forehead on them wearily.

The woman had fed them. A good meal—soup, mutton, and cheese, the best he'd had since they left Sarres, and despite his worry he had been hungry for it. She'd cooked it in the old kitchen below, where broken spits hung askew under the vast sooty throats of the chimneys, and she'd waited while they'd eaten it. But even Raffi had sensed the stifled fear in her, heard the small, impatient creaks her chair had made. She was desperate to get out.

At last Galen had cut a slice of cheese with deliberate care and said, "When you go, lock the doors from the outside. Whatever sounds you hear, whatever strange sights you may see, you stay away. Neither you nor anyone else is to come back to this house until full daylight. Do you understand that?"

Relieved, she had nodded, but at the door had turned and said, hesitating, "I could take the boy with me. Is it right to put the boy in danger?"

Galen hadn't even looked up. "The boy is a scholar of the Order. How else will he learn?"

When she'd gone, they'd come up here, to the highest rooms; Galen had taken his time choosing this one. Raffi broke mud-clots off his boots nervously. He wished he were back on Sarres, or anywhere, even at the fair. At least that had been out in the open; he could breathe or run. Here he felt as if the ancient house was stifling him, all its shutters tight, the carpet of dust, the webs, the mildewed walls. It was quiet, all the sense-lines were still, but there was something wrong with them, bizarrely wrong—they were warped, as if something else was here inside them, bulging them out.

He wondered if Galen could feel it too.

Now the Relic Master sat back on his heels, the hook of his nose shadowed. Without looking at Raffi he said, "You knew a keeper was among the prisoners, didn't you?"

Raffi clenched his fists. He'd been waiting for this.

"I heard something," he muttered.

"And you didn't tell me."

"I thought you'd have heard it too."

Galen glared at him. "And if I hadn't? You'd have waited till they were dead, would you, before you cared to mention it?"

Raffi looked away, hot.

"For Flain's sake, Raffi, when will you learn to have faith!" Galen's fury was always sudden, an explosion of temper. "All the study you've done, all the things you've seen! Can't you understand yet that the Makers are guiding us? We weren't called to this place by accident! It's not coincidence that one of the few keepers left alive is one of their prisoners. This is Flain's will, as clearly as if he appeared and told us "Rescue them!"

He tugged the dirty string out of his hair angrily. "And you try and ignore it!"

"Because I never know what you'll do," Raffi said despairingly.

Galen laughed, scornful. "Rubbish. You know very well. And that's what scares you."

He rubbed a dusty hand through his hair, scattering the remnants of ash. Raffi was silent. He knew it was true. Bitter shame broke out in him. "Perhaps I'm not fit to be a keeper," he snapped, his face hot.

Galen snorted. "That's for me to say. I haven't wasted all this time on you for nothing. You'll be a keeper if I have to beat it into you. Now pick up that lamp. We need to look at this house."

Raffi scrambled up and snatched the lamp. He wanted to march out with it boldly, down the stairs, into all the dark corridors, flinging open the doors, as fearless as Carys would have been. But he knew he'd falter at the first corner. In some ways learning the powers of the Order, sensing Maker-life in the land, the energy fields of people's dreams, of trees and stones and creatures, just made things worse. Carys couldn't feel all that. Perhaps that was why it was easy for her not to be scared.

Though Galen never was either.

As the keeper walked out onto the dark landing, Raffi followed him close. Together they looked over the banister, seeing the vast stairwell curl down into blackness, its walls stained with slow-growing lichens and the velvety mounds of mold that spread like vivid green stars.

Below, in the emptiness, nothing moved.

They could hear water dripping. Then a shutter banged. The house seemed immense, a labyrinth of rooms and courtyards and sculleries, buried in drifts of dust and memories, its timbers worm-gnawed and decaying. Raffi sent delicate sense-lines into it, infiltrating the whole tilted structure, scaring the slender-legged harvestmen that scuttled from its ceilings. Two floors below, a rat sneaked from a sooty hearth into a hole. The farther down his third eye searched, the uneasier it made him. Just as he was getting dizzy Galen said, "Stay close. Keep the lines out."

They went down, step after step. The lamp sent vast wobbling shadows up the walls. On each floor, Galen walked stealthily along the corridors, opening doors, gazing into chambers that were empty but for a fireplace and high windows, mostly patched and shuttered. But outside a room on the first floor he paused, his fingers on the handle. Raffi felt it too, the faintest shiver of Maker-power. Galen glanced at him.

Then he went in.

The room was black. In the doorway, Raffi held up the lamp.

To his astonishment a small circle of flowers lay on the bare boards. There was nothing else. No one stood in the shadowed corners, though as he moved the lamp, vast darknesses flickered and jerked.

After a second, Galen went and kneeled over the garland, Raffi close behind, glad to shut the door.

The flowers were yellow; they were the sort known as Flainscrown, as bright and fresh as if they'd just been picked. Raffi stared in amazement. "Where did they come from? It's winter!"

Galen turned a frail stem in his fingers. "They've been put here in the last few minutes."

Rooms below, something slammed. Raffi froze, listening so intently it hurt. Then he whispered, "What if it gets upstairs?"

"That's what I want. The awen-beads will draw it to the top room . . . Haven't I taught you the spiral yet?"

Raffi shook his head.

Oddly stiff, Galen's voice said, "Shine that light back here."

The Flainscrown was withering. Even as they watched, the leaves dried up, the petals turned brown and flaked into dust. Galen held nothing but a dry stem. He snapped it thoughtfully.

"What does it mean?"

The keeper gave him a sidelong look. "I don't know. Yet." Outside, Galen turned left, but as Raffi closed the door his eyes caught a scuttle of movement on the stair.

"There! Look!"

The lamp shook, sending shadows flying. Galen grabbed his shoulder fiercely. "For God's sake, keep quiet!"

Around them the house rang with the cry, agitated, like a still pool broken by a stone. All the ends of Raffi's nerves quivered; he felt cold, instantly cold.

After a moment Galen said, "What was it?"

"A . . . small thing." Raffi gripped the warm handle of the lamp with both hands to steady it. "It . . . crept."

"A rat?"

"Bigger." His heart was thudding like a pain. Galen didn't move, as if part of him was reaching out, sensing. Then he said, "It's coming. We'd better get back up there."

Quietly they ran up the broad wooden staircase, and all the way Raffi felt the stirring in the house, the slow gathering of something far below, its energies twisting up the smooth balustrades, the invisible carved cornices high above his head.

In the top room Galen propped the door open, snatched the lamp, and put it in the center of the beads, its light opening a complex net of seven spirals, jet and green, small emerald sparks glinting in the dark. He pulled Raffi close, inside the pattern, and the raw tension of the Crow scorched, so that Raffi jerked away, breathless.

"Keep still!" Galen hissed.

Far below, something was coming. They couldn't hear it but they could feel it; a pulsing energy, unformed yet, gathering itself out of cellars and deep courses of brickwork. It rose up along passageways, through halls, all the time knitting together, clotting into a swirling flux that crowded Raffi's sense-lines so that he could barely breathe, and had to crouch down over the sharp stitch in his side.

Closer. Now the whole house creaked with it, as if it drew itself in filaments of darkness out of all the wooden stairs and warped doors, ran in trickles down the damp walls. And it breathed; he could hear its breathing, and its footsteps as it climbed. Staring in dread at the black rectangle of the open door he clutched his coat in tight fistfuls, feeling Galen draw himself up beside him.

The keeper was intent. A soft, rich scent filled the room, the muskiness of decay.

Then, in the doorway, a shape moved. Raffi saw it through the glow of the awen-spiral, a presence lurking out there in the dark.

"Closer," Galen said. "Come closer."

Slow, reluctant, it slid into the room, huge and dark, all the desolation of the house held in a loose human outline, featureless and blurred, as if it might break down at any time, might flood out.

Galen held his hand up. "Enough."

It stopped.

Shivering, Raffi pulled back, shook off sense-lines. He didn't want to feel it; the stink of it in his nostrils sickened him.

"Why are you still here?" Galen asked softly.

The outline blurred. A gap like a mouth opened in the smooth face. "This is unfair," it hissed. Its voice was hoarse and crude; a patchwork of echoes and creaks and overheard whispers. "I wanted to go. He awakened me."

"Who awakened you?"

"He did."

"Do you want to be at peace?"

Frost Fair

"Let me. Let me go. Into the dark."

It squirmed, its outline breaking down, the body running and dissolving suddenly into a black pool, trickling and spreading over the floor to the very edge of the spiral. Small black fingers touched the beads and jerked back.

"In the name of Flain," Galen said quietly, "I dissolve you and absolve you. In the names of Soren and Tamar I release the pain from you . . ."

The pool bubbled. Out of it rose a great mass of tentacles that soared and groped high over their heads. Raffi ducked with a yelp of fear but Galen's voice went on, relentless. "In the name of Theriss I draw out your dark dreams. In the name of Halen I unfasten you, atom by atom. And in the name of Kest—"

The creature screamed. It slithered itself up into manshape and howled, arms overhead, bending and swaying as if in agony. The beads crackled and spat. Galen glanced at them anxiously.

"Not that name!" The voice broke into hisses of static, barely understandable. "Not him! He started it! The terror, the decay!" It squirmed into separate flames of blackness, wordless moans, then hurled itself forward at them, hands out.

Raffi leaped back; Galen lashed out and grabbed him.

"Still!" he snarled.

The awen-beads sparked. Smoke filled the room, blurring the light. The creature impacted on the invisible barrier and spread like a blot. It swarmed around them, hung over their heads, a black mass of despair. Raffi could feel its agony like a weight. He was dizzy, his chest ached.

"Let me finish!" Galen said.

"No! Not that name!"

"The Litany . . ."

"*You* must do it," the voice howled. "I know who you are. I know the Crow. Let me go to them through you!"

Astounded, Raffi turned. The voice was everywhere— in his head, filling his veins. Back to back with Galen they were both swallowed in blackness, the lamplight gone as if some great beast had devoured it.

"It's too dangerous," Galen muttered.

"Please! Trust me!" It squirmed piteously. "I have

been evil, done evil. Let me have peace, keeper."

Galen cursed bitterly. Then he dropped Raffi's arm. In the darkness his face was gaunt, eyes black. "Stay in the spiral," he hissed.

"Galen!"

It was useless. The keeper pushed him aside and stepped over the beads, into blackness.

4

Evil is a shadow.
Without light it could not exist.

Litany of the Makers

THE ROOM LAUGHED.

A deep, devilish chuckle. Raffi felt dismay well up in him; he shuddered, saying blind, meaningless phrases from the Litany over and over.

For a second he couldn't see Galen at all; the keeper was eaten by the murk. And then, gradually, it rolled up, dragged back, shriveled into the vast shadow of a man, face-to-face with Galen, fingertip to fingertip.

The keeper stood tall; he had the crackling stillness about him that was the Crow; his hair dark and glossy, the very air about him riven with sudden threads of energy. He spread his hands; the shadow-hands spread too, as if the creature were somehow the reverse of the keeper.

"Come to the Makers. Let yourself come." It was a harsh voice, barely Galen's, making Raffi think of vast distances, the emptiness between stars. But to his surprise the creature's reply was calm and amused.

"No," it said. "You come to me, keeper. Come to the dark."

Galen stared.

The featureless face stared back.

In the bare lamplit room they confronted each other, both charged with power. Catching the awen-beads at his neck Raffi saw the invisible struggle between them, knew the shadow-creature was growing, swelling into strength.

"Come to me, keeper," it said again, and now its fingers were locked in Galen's, trapping them tight, pulling him close. "You've always wanted to. Deep into the dark."

Galen didn't answer. Silence raged between them, as if their souls ebbed and flowed in a bitter tussle channeled through fingertips and sense-lines. When Raffi tried to reach out to help, the ferocity of it flung him back.

"Galen!" he cried.

The keeper was fading, flooded by darkness.

"Galen!"

"Darkness is stronger," the creature hissed. "It was first, and will be last. Enter it with me."

"Who . . . awakened you?" Galen had to force the words out.

"He did. The one you fear. The Great One."

"The Great One? Who is that?"

Suddenly the creature tried to jerk away. Galen gripped it tight. "Is it the one called the Margrave? Does he control you? Did he send you here?"

"Let me stay!" It was a howl, a scream, and with sudden panic the shadow fought, but Galen pulled it closer.

"I can't go to the Makers," it sobbed. "I've been evil."

"No one is turned away. No one." Galen's fingers merged into the black hands, warm as fire. He hugged it into himself. "Come to us," he said.

And to Raffi's astonishment the creature's blackness had stars in it, distant suns and tiny nebulae, and then it was fading, passing into the keeper's fingers, into his body and beyond him, far out to somewhere else, streaming into the sense-lines and the stars, still crying out, still sobbing.

Until it was gone.

THE LAMP FLICKERED. Galen was alone.

For a second he stood there; then he muttered, "Raffi," and staggered back. Raffi grabbed him; together they crumpled breathless onto the bare boards.

Galen dragged in breath. His hair was soaked with sweat, his face white as if in pain. Raffi looked around for water but there was none.

"The beads," the keeper croaked. "Give me the beads."

The spiral was broken, all its green and black crystals scattered, as if something had blasted them wide. Raffi gathered up a handful and pressed them into Galen's fingers; the keeper held them tight, bending over, forcing himself to breathe, to be calm, and as his eyes opened, just for an instant, Raffi was sure he saw the echoes of tiny stars fade out of their blackness.

Unless it was the lamp.

"What did you do?"

"I don't know." Galen leaned back against the wall, his breathing ragged. He looked exhausted.

"You asked it about the Margrave."

"Yes." The keeper looked up. Rubbing his cheek with the edge of his palm he said, "Something's not right here. That was no ghost, no trapped relic-power. That was real, malevolent, a creature woken, maybe even made intentionally."

"To do what?"

Galen shrugged. "To get us here."

Raffi went cold. "Us?"

"A keeper. Any keeper. Bait."

Raffi chewed his nails. "If that's true, we ought to get away."

"Not before we stop those executions."

There was silence a moment, a hostile, worried silence. Then the keeper said, "I need some water. Go and get it. And anything she left to eat. Bring the pack up too."

Reluctant, Raffi scrambled to his feet.

"You won't need the lamp," Galen said wearily,

watching him reach for it. "The house is empty. Feel it."

And all down the stairs he could feel it, a silence raw and astonished.

When he came back they ate the rest of the cheese. Galen drank heavily and then spread the blanket over his legs and leaned back, closing his eyes.

"I don't understand," Raffi muttered. "Why did it put the flowers there?"

"It didn't."

Puzzled, he chewed the hard rind. "We saw them."

"We saw them. But that creature didn't put them there."

"So who did?"

But Galen did not answer.

BANGING WOKE HIM. A hard, insistent banging that seemed to go on and on, until Raffi rolled over with a groan and heard Galen unbolting the doors below. Echoes of a woman's voice murmured in the house.

He sat up.

Bleak gray light was seeping through the boarded

windows. He yawned and scratched and rubbed his face with dry hands. Then he pulled his boots on and went downstairs.

In the kitchen they were talking.

The woman had a bundle in her arms; she laid it on the table. "Are you sure?" she said, dubious, looking around.

Galen was tired and bad-tempered. "It's gone. It won't be back."

Raffi was amazed she couldn't feel that. The whole house was calm around him, as if it had slept for the first time in weeks. He knew that was why he felt so bleary.

She nodded. "I'll have to take your word. I've brought these, but if anyone asks me, mind, they were stolen. I never saw you or want to know anything about what you do with them."

Galen opened the bundle. It contained dark clothes, a few small silver discs on a chain, and some papers.

"They may not fit you," she warned.

He looked up. "I'll take a chance. We'll leave now. We need to get there in time."

"But what about food? I have to thank you, and the boy looks famished."

"The boy always looks famished," he snapped, going out. They heard him limping up the stairs.

Majella turned to Raffi. The morning light showed the wrinkles in her skin, the graying hair. "What happened?" she asked, fascinated. "He looks worn out. What was in here?"

He knew better than to say too much. "A sort of . . . energy. Probably left over from some relic. Galen said the incarnations and we prayed. It just faded out."

He was poor at lying. She looked at him closely. "I see. And now, what does he want these clothes for? If it's for what I think, then he's crazy! He'll never get away with it!"

"The Makers will help us," Raffi muttered.

"If he's killed," she said, "and you're on your own, come back. I'll hide you."

Astonished, he looked at her.

She glanced away. "My lad used to look a bit like you. When he was young."

Galen shouldered his way in, the pack in his arms. He dumped the peddler's empty tray on the table. "Burn that."

Frost Fair

"Don't worry." She pushed a small sacking roll at Raffi. "That's food. Eat it in the cart. And thank you for coming here, keeper. Now we can make something of the place."

He looked at her. "Did your son know about this haunting?"

"Not from me. The men may have said something. Now, are you certain you want to go back to the fair?"

Galen did up the straps of the pack. "Certain."

"Keeper—"

He looked up. She was watching him anxiously.

"I don't ask. But if there's . . ." She shook her head. "I mean, you have weapons, powers. I don't understand them. But I have only one son, and all I ask is that he's not hurt."

Galen looked at her in surprise. Then he said, "Mistress, you have great faith. Far more than you think."

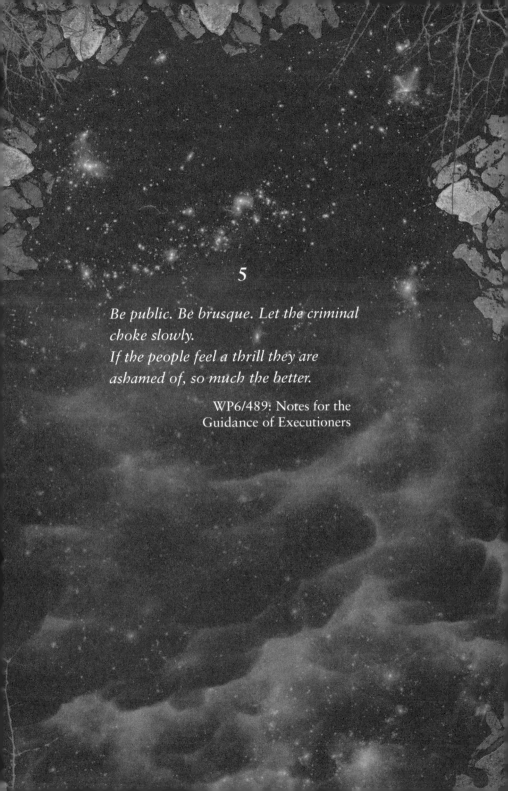

5

*Be public. Be brusque. Let the criminal
choke slowly.*
*If the people feel a thrill they are
ashamed of, so much the better.*

WP6/489: Notes for the
Guidance of Executioners

EVERYONE WAS WAITING.

Shoving his way through the crowd, Raffi could feel the tension. Today the fair was full, crammed to bursting, and the noise was intolerable—loud talk, forced laughter, intense bargaining—as if people tried to drown out the fear inside themselves or argue it away. Music seemed sharper in the cold air. He was lightheaded with it all, his own terror a chill down his spine. Even the animals, sheep and marsets and boshorns, bleated and fidgeted and racked their stalls with restless energy, hooves chipping the frozen floor into tiny drifts of snow that the wind gusted into corners.

Out in the center of the solid lake the gallows waited too, black and gaunt. Around them stood a ring of armed Watchmen, faces muffled against the icy wind. One of them, he prayed, must be Galen.

They had separated outside the checkpoints, and Raffi had come in first with the pack—easy enough, as the crush had been fierce. Were they all so keen to watch people die? he thought in disgust. Or was it that the Watch would notice anyone who stayed away?

Already the front row of the crowd was pressing against the ropes, finding good places. Sellers of sausages and ale and hot cakes were doing a fast trade. Raffi chewed his thumbnail, anxious. Had Galen gotten in? Or had he been arrested already? He narrowed his eyes against the sleety wind and tried to see, but each Watchman was tall and dark and he could feel nothing from them. They all had crossbows too. Where would Galen have gotten one?

If the keeper was captured, then it was up to him. He squashed that thought away. There was nothing he could do on his own.

Then, like a cold touch, he felt something. A brush of knowledge, the edge of it like a feather against his mind.

Frost Fair

Someone was watching him.

He turned. Around him the stalls were busy. He saw coopers, blacksmiths, singers, all sorts of peddlers and hucksters and hawkers, a man with a dancing bear, a gang of girl beggars. None of them seemed to have noticed him. He walked away quickly, weaving in and out of the crowd, anxious to lose himself, his heart thumping. It might have been Galen. That thought washed over him with relief, but still he sent a few sense-lines out, feeling instantly only the confusion of the crowd, its dizzying desires and anxieties and laughter.

Then the drumming began.

At once people surged forward, Raffi pushed along with them. Bargaining was abandoned; men and women elbowed for position, a better view. He tried to worm his way out, edging down the rope toward the nearest point to the gallows, as Galen had told him to.

The prisoners were coming out. They were filthy and bruised. Ten of them. Five men, two women, and three bedraggled-looking Sekoi, all with their hands tied loosely in front.

The crowd went quiet. Only the drums thudded like a

heartbeat. Raffi looked carefully along the stumbling line, seeing an old woman, a young, white-faced boy. When he came to the third man, his gaze fixed, all the hairs on the backs of his hands stirring. He knew this was the keeper.

He was an elderly man, straight-backed, silver hair swept back to the nape of his neck, his face calm, despite its dirt and bruises. A smooth, noble face. He wore a long, ragged gray coat. Power was all around him; even Raffi could sense it. The others were terrified, yet this man felt nothing but compassion; Raffi saw how he turned to a bald, thickset prisoner behind him, obviously injured, and put an arm around his shoulders. Ignoring the angry yell of the Watch commander, he supported the man across the slippery ice, speaking to him quietly.

Raffi bit his lip. He had no idea what Galen was planning. It would be reckless; Galen always was. But how could they ever hope to get away, unless it was to try and lose themselves in the crowd?

The drums stopped.

Dead silence.

The prisoners gathered in a huddle, the silver-haired man looking out at the crowd. His eyes seemed to scan their faces, as if he was alert, sensing something. Raffi ducked under a woman's arm and crouched in the front. The Watchguards held their bows ready, facing the crowd.

The first to be hanged was a woman; young, barely out of her teens. As two Watchmen dragged her forward she turned to the silver-haired keeper, arms stretched out. He put his hand out and gripped hers, then blessed her, the sign of Flain made clear and proud.

Around Raffi, the crowd seemed to become stiller, totally silent. The nearest Watchman fidgeted with his bow, his eyes nervous over the dark scarf that covered his face.

The woman was forced to the gallows. Above her the black ropes swung in the icy wind; she glanced up at them once. Raffi felt sick and panicky. He wanted to turn away, not to see. Where was Galen? What if he wasn't even here?

Someone in the crowd yelled something. A guard aimed his bow ominously. The girl was pushed up onto the first step. She cried out, a great gasp of terror.

And at that instant Raffi felt a quiver under his feet, a faint vibration in the frozen lake growing quickly, forcibly; a tension building up like the pressure of a blocked waterspout. He glanced down, sensing with sudden amazement what Galen must be doing; then he was running, ducking under the ropes, dodging the guard, racing over the ice toward the gallows.

The crowd sent up a yell. Crossbows swiveled. One bolt shot past him and skittered over the frozen lake, but he was already at the gallows, almost with the prisoners.

And the ice heaved!

He fell, sliding on hands and knees, sprawled.

Behind him, the lake shattered with an earsplitting crack. Plates of ice tilted up, sharp-fanged. The Watchmen toppled, grabbed each other to stay upright. Between them and the prisoners a vast crevasse was opening, a gaping black chasm in the ice, and the whole surface under the fair was shuddering up. Booths and stands went crashing; terrified bulls trampled out of their stalls. People were shouting, screaming.

The prisoners stood as if in shock; then the silver man whirled suddenly, barging into the guard behind, knocking him off his feet.

Raffi tried to stand.

"Galen!" he yelled.

Frost Fair

"Get him, Raffi! Get him to the forest!"

The voice was close, in his head. Scrambling up he raced over and shoved the other guard hard in the back, sending the raised crossbow out of his hands and whirling across the ice. One of the Sekoi dived after it.

The keeper had the guard's knife; he was slicing the ropes. Crossbow bolts clattered around him. From the Watchtower a brazen horn rang out.

The keeper looked up. "Where?" was all he said.

"The forest," Raffi gasped.

The keeper caught the bald man, who waved him off feebly. "Leave me! Just get clear!"

"Oh no, my son. Not while there's a soul to save." With an effort he heaved the man up. "Go on!" he yelled.

Raffi ran. The lake was slipping away under him; the fringes of the forest seemed miles away. Furious yells behind them terrified him. The chasm must be wide, he knew, but he could already hear stalls being torn down, wood slammed on the ice. And still the lake buckled, splitting with enormous cracks, so that he went sprawling with the aftershocks, the surface crumpling beneath his feet.

He glanced back. The two men were close. All the other prisoners had already scattered; he saw a Sekoi firing a crossbow and another lying still on the ice. Panic-stricken sheep were rampaging among the wreckage of the fair, but that was far away. And where was Galen?

Ahead, the forest loomed, the vast quenta trees spreading their roots far under the frozen water. Raffi scrambled through frosted reeds and turned to help. "I'm all right," the bald man snapped, but the pain in his arms and shoulders shimmered out of him; Raffi caught the edge of it and gasped.

They fell over tree roots, the gloom of the forest enclosing them. A little way in, the keeper stopped. He eased the bald man down and spun around, breathless.

"Followers," he gasped. "Need to deal with them."

A twig cracked. Someone was close on their trail, and rounding the trees a Watchman came, low under the branches, the crossbow armed in his hands. He stopped instantly and said, "It's all right. It's me."

Raffi grinned with relief.

Galen pulled the dark wrappings off his face.

"Can you still run?" he asked quickly.

Frost Fair

The two men nodded, silent with surprise. Then the tall one said, "My name is Solon. This is Marco. Who are you?"

"That can wait." Galen grabbed the bald man and hauled him up. "We have to get farther in," he said anxiously. "They've got razorhounds."

Raffi went cold.

Far back over the shattered lake, terrible snarls rang out.

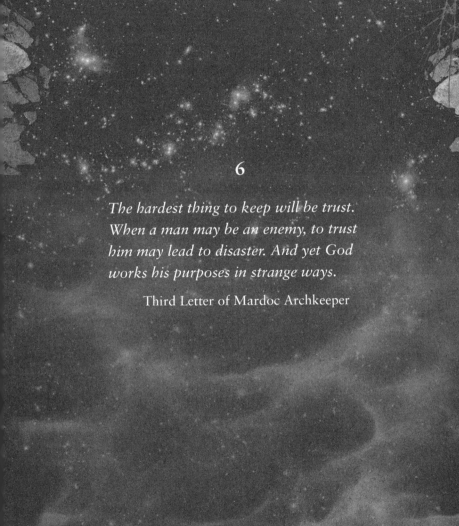

6

*The hardest thing to keep will be trust.
When a man may be an enemy, to trust
him may lead to disaster. And yet God
works his purposes in strange ways.*

Third Letter of Mardoc Archkeeper

T HE QUENTA FOREST was said to stretch for miles, but only after a few minutes the tangle of vast trunks became impassable. Branches knotted together, split and interlaced. There was no way through. Paths led in circles back to the lake.

The fugitives ran till they were breathless, then crouched against the bole of a king-quenta, the man called Marco clutching his shoulder in agony.

"How far have we gone?" Raffi gasped.

"Not far enough." Galen threw down the crossbow, dragged the black gloves off, and hurled them angrily into the knotted darkness. "We need to speak to the trees. Get them to let us through."

He turned quickly to Solon. "Will you do that?"

The older man stared back, his face calm, his blue eyes shrewd and deep. "I would be able to, if I were one of the Order."

"There's no time for that," Galen snapped. "I know you are."

"Do you?"

"So am I. You can feel that, can't you?"

Solon's stare was even. Then to Raffi's horror he said, "No. What I sense about you is strange and utterly dark. Not like any keeper I may ever have met. I'm sorry," he said, half turning. "I can't take the risk."

What he did Raffi barely saw. There was a crack of light. Galen staggered back with a gasp of pain. Then he was down, crumpled against the tree roots. Still.

"Galen?" Raffi whispered.

A rustle made him turn. The bald man, Marco, had the crossbow. Painfully he aimed it at Galen's head.

"NO!"

Raffi ran forward, right in front of the tense bolt.

"How can you do this?" he yelled, wild with fury. "We got you out of there! We helped you to escape!"

"The ice cracked. And we ran," Solon said.

"But Galen did that! He cracked the ice!"

"I'm not a fool, my son," the man said mildly. "No keeper, not even the most learned, could do that on his own. He's part of some Watchplan. For all I know, so are you."

"I'm his scholar!"

"I'm sure you are. Keep the other one covered, Marco." Briskly, almost kindly, he came and tied up Raffi's hands and feet with the ends of rope, then with a strip torn from his shirt gagged him gently and pushed him over. Raffi sat down hard next to Galen.

Solon crouched. "I've been a prisoner of the Watch for a long time," he said, his voice strangely quiet. "I'm never going back alive. You might be spies—I can't take the risk. You may also be what you say. If so, I pray to Flain to forgive me. And that they don't find you." Turning, he said, "Come on."

He took the bald man's arm over his shoulder, sagging a little with the weight. "You should leave the bow."

Marco grinned. "Good try, Your Holiness. Maybe later." He clutched it tight, like a crutch.

Then they were gone, lost in the tangle of quenta trees like shadows, the only sound a rustle and a cracked twig.

Raffi kicked and struggled. Furiously he squirmed around onto his side and nudged Galen with his tied feet, then shoved harder, trying to call the keeper's name. Only stupid muffled sounds came out.

Far off, where the lake must be, a razorhound howled. Another answered it. Galen didn't move. Raffi tugged his wrists frantically, feeling the tight bonds scorch his skin. Then, deliberately, he lay still and opened his third eye.

He was tired and scared, and it was an effort. But after two minutes' forced concentration he managed to make a small circle of light and let his mind crawl through it, into a room. Dimly he recognized it, the lamp, the bare, dusty floorboards. Galen lay here, crumpled and still, one arm flung out. But now there were flowers scattered on him, over his back and hair and all around him, the fresh strange yellow flowers of Flainscrown. Raffi brushed them off hastily, grabbing the keeper's shoulder.

"Galen!" he said. "Wake up!"

Galen's eyes snapped open. He rolled over, looked around at the room and the flowers, picked one up. "These again?" he muttered.

And suddenly they were back in the quenta forest, and in his fingers there was only a shriveled leaf.

"Raffi!" Instantly the keeper was on his feet. He rolled Raffi over, whipped off the gag, and fumbled for a knife. "What happened?"

"Solon. He used the Third Action. Thinks we're Watch." Raffi wriggled out of the ropes hurriedly. "They can't have gone far. Are we going after them?"

"Of course we are!" Galen's eyes were black with annoyance. "He's a keeper! We need him!"

"But if he won't believe us . . ."

"I'll make him." Galen hauled him up roughly and grabbed the pack. "Go on! Quickly!"

They hurried, following broken leaves, branches. There was no need for anything more; the trail was only too obvious. Behind them the razorhounds snarled and spat, answering each other across the lake, always closer.

Galen burst through a hanging curtain of leaves, Raffi

breathless behind. The keeper stopped dead; peering past him, Raffi saw why.

Solon was kneeling, deep in the leaves. He wasn't touching the tree, but they could feel his contact with it, his struggle to reach its deep intelligence.

Galen stepped forward. To his left, a crossbow swiveled up.

"My God, you're persistent!" Marco muttered.

"He needs me to help him. Or none of us will get out of this." Without moving from where he stood, Galen sent sudden sense-lines of energy flickering between the trees, their power raw and sharp. Instantly Solon glanced back. He looked amazed, then afraid.

"Who are you?" he breathed.

But Galen spoke to the forest. "Let us through," he said quietly. "Make a way and close it after us. The men behind us are despoilers, burners of trees. We need to escape from them. Will you do this for us?"

Like the stirring of many leaves the forest answered him, its voice rustling and multifold. *It has been many years.*

"I know that. But you see who we are."

Frost Fair

We see. You are Soren's Sons.

Raffi was surprised. It was a name for the Order rarely heard now, written only once or twice in very old books, like the Prophecies of Askelon.

Something dragged and slithered next to him, so that he turned in fear. Branches and leaves were drawing back. Beyond them was a dim green darkness.

We make a way for you, the wood whispered. *Go through.*

The hole led deep into the forest. It was a network of spaces, the knotted boughs easing apart, leaving gaps to scramble through and over; far in front of them Raffi could see it unfurling, a dim tunnel of branches. He went in front, pushing and climbing. Galen came next with Marco, Solon was last, and behind him with scarcely a sound the trees closed their mesh again, the giant branches sprouting and interlocking.

Down here the gloom was so deep nothing else grew, only pale toadstools and ghostly threads of fungus fingering up from the accumulated springy mattresses of a century's dead leaves. Stumbling, Raffi remembered Galen once telling him that the quenta forest was supposed to be all one tree, a vast, sprawling entity. If that was the case, they were deep inside its body now, miles inside, the smooth green-lichened trunks rising above him into rustling canopies.

After what seemed an age Galen gasped, "All right, Raffi. This is enough."

It was a small clearing, musty-smelling. When Raffi sat down he sank into leaves to his waist, dry and crumbling.

Galen, limping now, eased Marco down. The bald man still held the crossbow. Leaning over, one hand on a tree bole, Galen dragged in deep breaths. He looked haggard, as if his old leg wound ached, but his eyes were sharp with that reckless triumph Raffi knew only too well. When Solon caught up, they were all silent a while, recovering. Raffi lay on his back and listened to the forest, the cold wind making an endless whistling in the high leaves above him, though down here everything was still, as if it had never moved. Lichen grew thick on trunks and bark; hanging green beards of it, as if snow or wind never penetrated, never disturbed it. Only the slow drip of the rain would reach this place.

Slowly the terror died in him. They were safe here. No

one else might ever have come this far in, not since the Makers walked the world.

Solon must have thought so too. He sat down wearily and looked up at Galen, rubbing one hand through his smooth silver hair. "It seems we have much to thank you for." Then he stood up abruptly and held out his hand.

Galen took it, their fingers tight in the sign of Meeting.

"Another keeper," Solon breathed. "I hardly believed there were any left!"

"A few."

"Flainsteeth," Marco muttered. "More fanatics."

Solon smiled at him. "Excuse my friend. He is something of an unbeliever. But still I have to say I don't understand how you could do all this."

Galen looked at him sidelong. "When we get to Sarres, I'll explain everything. Not before. We may still be captured."

"Sarres!" Solon's eyes went wide with intense curiosity. "Sarres is a lost place! A place in legend!"

Galen smiled a wolfish smile. "That's what you think," he said.

Mardoc's Ring

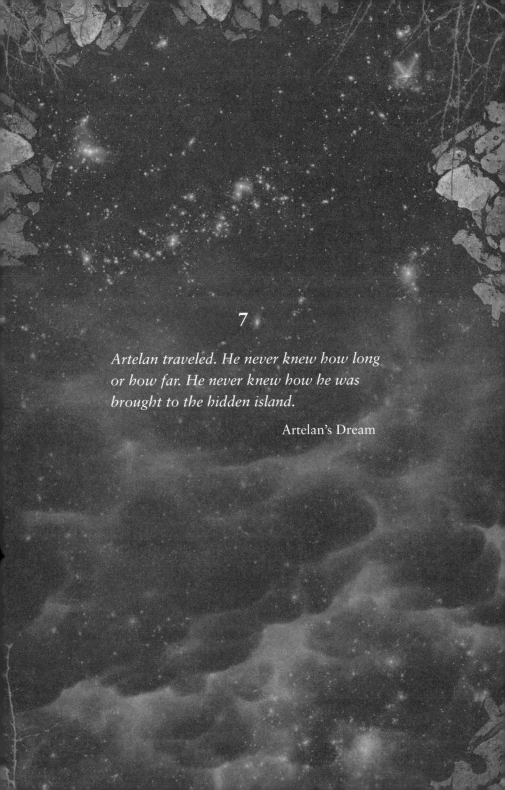

7

Artelan traveled. He never knew how long or how far. He never knew how he was brought to the hidden island.

Artelan's Dream

CARYS PUT THREE CARDS DOWN carefully. "Crescent," she muttered.

Sitting cross-legged opposite her on the grass the Sekoi smiled. Its seven fingers plucked out an Emperor and pushed it carelessly into the last gap in the ring.

"Circle," it said smugly.

Carys swore. "You can't have!"

"I have." The creature smirked, its yellow eyes bright. With both hands it gathered the great pile of withered chestnuts toward itself. "So all these are mine. I make that four thousand gold marks exactly that you owe me."

Disgusted, Carys flung the cards down. "You were cheating. You had to be cheating!"

"Prove it."

"You deal too fast."

"Skill," the creature said, crunching one of the nuts. "And these." It waved its fingers at her.

Carys leaned back against the calarna tree, folding her arms. "You know you'll never see the money."

"I live in hope. But I would have thought that a Watchspy would have been able to teach me a few tricks in card-sharping. What do you people do in your time off?"

"There isn't any." Carys brushed the blown hair from her eyes irritably. She didn't want to think about the Watch, let alone discuss it. But she said, "And I'm not a Watchspy. Not anymore."

"Ah." The Sekoi looked over the smooth lawns of Sarres to the house, and the strange green hill beyond. Geese wandered under the trees, pecking at grass. "My people have a saying. 'Darkness is a stain that will not wash away.'"

Carys's eyes went hard. "Meaning?"

Idly it stroked the tribemark on its furred face. When

it looked at her again its eyes were sly. "I think you know I've never been quite sure of you, Carys," it said quietly.

She laughed bitterly. "Only too well. What do I have to do to convince you? Isn't it enough to be on every death-list for miles?"

The Sekoi lounged elegantly on the grass. "Ah, but I know the Watch. Anyone can be on a list. Anyone can seem to be an outlaw, and still be working undercover."

"Galen trusts me. And Galen—"

"Is the Crow. I know. He is also a man wholly possessed by his faith. Sometimes I think that makes him blind to danger. Certain dangers."

They looked at each other in silence, Carys hot with annoyance. In the stillness the birdsong seemed louder. The endless ripple of the hidden spring, Artelan's Well itself, bubbled from under the yew trees.

When she spoke again her voice was spiteful. "Time will tell."

The Sekoi closed its eyes against the sun. "Indeed. I will be watching."

"So will I, Graycat. Because the Sekoi would sell their only sons for a bent button. That's an old saying too."

As it opened one eye and stared at her, surprised, the door of the house flew open and Felnia ran out, racing wildly over the grass, her short hair flying. She flung her arms wide.

"They're coming! The Guardian says they're coming!"

Carys scrambled up, the Sekoi tall beside her. "Now?"

"Soon. Any time!" The little girl was breathless with delight, her face somehow smeared with soil from the gardens. Behind her the Guardian, Tallis, came slowly, in her old-woman shape, wiping her hands on her dress. She looked uneasy, her face tense with worry. "They're not alone," she said as she came up.

Instantly Carys was wary. "Who's with them?"

"I don't know. More than one."

The Sekoi flicked her a glance. "We should be ready in case . . ."

"I'll get my bow. You go to the causeway."

Hurtling into the house and into the small room of sweet-smelling wood that was hers now, she rummaged in the corner chest anxiously. The bow had been in here since she came; there was no need for weapons on Sarres. But her Watchtraining was always sharp in her, so she'd kept it oiled and clean. Grabbing a handful of bolts, she racked the mechanism back and jammed one in.

It might be all right. Galen might have found some more of the Order. But all the time she knew only too well what else could have happened. The Watch had expert interrogators. They used pain relentlessly. There were no secrets left after the rack, after being hung by the wrists, and as much as she loved Raffi, she knew that he would never stand up against that.

Ferociously she pushed the thought away, ran down and out into the spring warmth of Sarres. At the edge of the lawn she raced through the trees and found the others waiting, the Sekoi firmly gripping Felnia's hand tight in its seven-fingered fist.

Before them stretched what seemed to be unbroken grass, but they knew this was illusion, the Maker-power that protected the sacred island. Beyond it a wicker causeway led through the marsh back to the Finished Lands, receding now each year. As she listened she heard a splash, faint voices.

"Whoever they are, say nothing in front of them about

what's happened," Tallis said quietly. "We can tell Galen and Raffi later. Understand, Felnia?"

The little girl nodded, impatient, her eyes fixed on the drifting mist.

It swirled open.

A faint smell came through, of woods and stagnant water, and a gust of icy wind that made Carys shiver.

She raised the bow.

Raffi was first. His face was almost hidden under a knotted rag of scarf, but he pulled it away with a whoop of delight and breathed deep, tasting the sweet air of the island. Then he grinned up at them. "Don't shoot. It's only us."

"Not only you." Carys paced forward warily. "Who else?"

"Friends. A keeper!" He crouched and opened his arms, and Felnia broke the Sekoi's grip and came running, flinging her arms around him, then punching and pummeling him until he fell over.

"Did you bring me anything from the fair? You said you would."

"I doubt they had the chance," Carys said drily.

She was disturbed by the change in him. After only three weeks outside he was tired and filthy and strained. The strain of long fear.

Then she looked behind him.

A man had come out of the mist, a stranger. His smooth hair was silver, matted with dirt. Around his eyes was tied a rag of scarf, so if Raffi had not turned to help him he would have stumbled, but then he straightened and stood still, stock-still, and she knew by the alert lift of his head he was using the things Raffi called sense-lines, feeling the warm grass, the fresh leaves on the trees.

"Incredible," he breathed.

"Where's Galen?" Carys asked.

"Here." The keeper shouldered out of the fog, dark and hook-nosed. With both hands he supported another man, bald, also blindfolded, clearly on the point of collapse. The Sekoi ran to him instantly, Tallis hurrying behind.

Carys stayed where she was, the bow unwavering.

With a gasp and a moan through gritted teeth, the bald man was gently lowered to the grass. He too had a crossbow, strapped to his back. Watch issue. Tallis kneeled beside him and tugged the blindfold off. He stared up at her in surprise.

Quickly she felt his arms and shoulders. "This man has been beaten."

Galen straightened, stiff and sore. "That's how the Watch treat their prisoners, Guardian." He looked around, his dark eyes moving gratefully over the trees and smooth lawns as if the beauty and order of it healed some deep inner hunger. "It's been a nightmare journey," he muttered.

The Sekoi glanced up. "Watch?"

"Everywhere. They know about the Crow."

Then he saw Carys and smiled his rare grim smile. "Not forgiven me yet?"

"Are you all right?" She lowered the bow and came down slowly.

"We are now. And these are friends."

"Are you sure?"

His smile faded and for a moment she caught that edge of strangeness that came and went in him, the darkness of the Crow. "As I can be. This is Solon."

He limped over and undid the blindfold gently, then took it away.

Carys saw how the man stiffened. He had a wise, experienced face under the dirt and bruises, lit up now with a sudden deep joy. He turned slowly, staring at the hill, the gardens, the house. "Dear God," he kept saying. "Dear God."

"Welcome to the lost land of Sarres," Galen said. "Now I think we should get Marco inside."

But Solon's hands shook; he clasped them tightly together. "All my life," he breathed, "I've dreamed and prayed for this."

He looked at Raffi in a kind of daze. "Is it real?"

Raffi grinned back wearily. "It's real."

How much of a nightmare the journey had been Carys could only guess. Raffi was too tired to talk; after he'd eaten, he fell asleep at the table, with Felnia leaning up against him. The man called Marco slept too, after the Guardian had given him some cordial. But Solon seemed too excited to be able to rest. He asked for some water, and when he came back later they could see that he had washed from head to toe; the skin on his arms and face was red, as if he had scrubbed and scrubbed. He wore clean clothes Tallis had brought for him. He went out, and from the window Carys watched him as the evening darkened and Agramon rose, wandering and touching and exploring until the lawns and lanes were dim and owls and were-birds called from the woods beyond. Then Galen and Tallis went out to him, taking candles.

They placed them on the grass and made him sit down, around the glow.

Above the trickle of the well she heard the three keepers chant the Night prayer, the strange Maker-syllables murmured under the ring of rising moons.

The Sekoi's shadow loomed at her shoulder.

"When should we tell him?" she muttered.

The creature made a small mew of unhappiness in its throat. "Tomorrow. Let them have one night in peace.

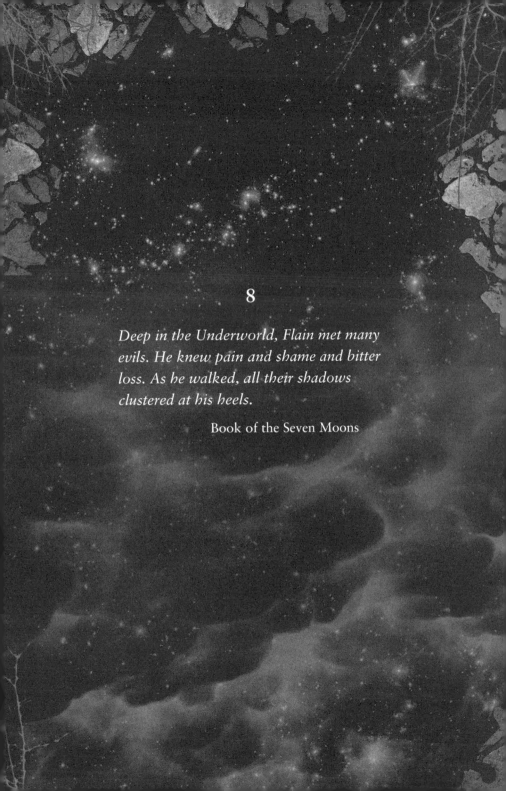

8

Deep in the Underworld, Flain met many evils. He knew pain and shame and bitter loss. As he walked, all their shadows clustered at his heels.

Book of the Seven Moons

"I'M THE STRANGER," Solon said quietly. "So I feel I should speak first."

They sat around the table in the great wooden room. From the garden the sun streamed in, lighting the tall images of Flain and Soren and Theriss in the colored glass of the windows. One shimmer lit Solon's hands and bony wrists, showing clearly the long, twisted scars.

"The choice is yours," Tallis said to him kindly. "No one expects it of you." Her shape had changed. Now she was a young woman, her long red hair plaited. He smiled at her.

"Yes, but I expect it. It will be a relief, in any case, to

be able to speak freely after so long." Looking around at their faces, he breathed out and said, "My friends, my full name is Solon Karner. I have been a Relic Master of the Order for over thirty years now. My master was Caradan Sheer of Tasceron. When I was very young, even before the Emperor fell, I studied with her at the Shrine of the Shells at Ranor."

"The shrine!" Galen looked impressed. "Were you there when it was burned?"

Solon's face went bleak. "I was seventeen." He paused, fingering a bruise on his face. "I remember the columns of the Watch riding up the hill to us, the running, the panic, books being snatched up, relics hidden. But there were so many relics there, how could we save them all? The beautiful gifts the Makers had left—precious things, never to be made again in all the ages of the world! I saw the Watch sear them with torches, rip down statues and smash them. None of us could believe they were doing this. I saw keepers fixed by crossbow bolts to the walls of their own shrine, heard their screams, saw the Makers' faces and hands hacked out and trampled. I saw such things there, my friends, that I prayed to God all my life for the power to forget them."

They were silent. Carys flicked a glance at Raffi, but he was looking desolately down at the table, away from her. Galen's face was set. In the next room, very faintly, they could hear Felnia chattering to Marco.

Solon took a deep breath. "It is so hard to forgive, Galen. Caradan was killed there. I had already made the Deep Journey, and I escaped. Sometimes that too is hard to forgive."

"The Makers needed you," Galen said gruffly.

"They did, my son." He gazed over at the bright glass image of Flain, standing with his hands out in the Field of Gold. "And yet I have sometimes wondered why they let me live. I am not greatly learned, not . . ." He smiled and shook his head. "Well. Enough of that. For years I worked alone, among the people. I gathered relics, prayed the Litany, fought the evils of Kest. I made copies of all the books I could remember, beautiful copies too, brilliantly colored, when I could beg the paper or make my own."

"What did you do with them?" the Sekoi asked curiously.

"The books? Gave them away, my friend. Many people hunger for knowledge of the Makers, now that the Watch have forbidden it. So much has been lost, so much destroyed."

The Sekoi nodded, but Carys noticed its baffled glance and almost grinned. "Where did you live?" she asked.

Solon looked at her. "In many places. It wasn't safe to stay anywhere long. Villages up in the Mara Kush, mostly, where people would hide me. I taught the children, held the feasts, worked with the trees and the land where such energies could still be reached. But relics were few and the Watch stronger every year. Also, Kest's work is growing. The Unfinished Lands spread; there are many famines and diseases. I helped at outbreaks of these. Once or twice, I was given the privilege of Healing."

Tallis looked at him closely. "That's a high gift, keeper. You say you made the Deep Journey. May I ask what branch of learning you reached?"

Solon shrugged. He seemed a little reluctant. After a moment he said, "The twelfth."

It obviously meant something. Raffi looked awestruck and Galen sat back, gazing at the keeper with dark eyes.

"That was a great achievement," he said, "for a man who is no scholar."

"My son, the Makers give. The achievement is theirs." Solon glanced sadly down at his scarred hands. "It was because of the Healing that I met Mardoc."

Carys jumped. Galen sat upright in excitement, his face edged with the reflected colors. "Mardoc the Eighth? The last Archkeeper!"

"The same."

"Where?"

"In a village not far from Tasceron, two days after the fall of the city."

They waited. He seemed unwilling to go on, as if the memory were a devastating one.

"Mardoc was hurt?" Tallis asked gently. "It is said he was carried from the city, after the great explosion."

"Yes. He was hurt. I thought that was why they sent for me." Rubbing his face with the edge of his hand he tried to keep his voice even. "It was a terrible night, there was deep snow. The Archkeeper lay in a ruined barn, out on the hills, in great agony. Only two scholars were with him. A villager fetched me, then fled. The Watch were everywhere, searching the farms, the villages, closing all the roads. The smoke of the Wounded City could be seen for miles; the terrible stench, the broken lines of power." He smiled wanly. "Mardoc knew the Watch would find him within the hour. One leg was shattered; he could go no farther. He ordered me to leave him and to take the two boys with me. He made me swear by the Book that I would take them and not look back."

He put his scarred fingers together, folding them tight. When he went on his voice was hoarse. "We prayed together. I offered him something for the pain, but he refused it. He wanted his mind clear. We both knew that he would be tortured without mercy."

"Then you should have killed him," Carys said.

Solon looked up at her in horror.

"Did he explain," the Sekoi put in hurriedly, "about what had happened in the city? About what had caused the great Darkness?"

"He said things. Meaningless phrases. Something about the fires, and Kest. He mentioned the Coronet of Flain."

"*What?*"

Mardoc's Ring

Galen and Tallis said it together, and their eyes met in surprise.

Solon was too absorbed in his memories to notice. "He was such a small man, gray and shrunken and old. But he had no fear, Galen, not even then. And he said to me—he put his hand on my shoulder and sent the boys outside and whispered to me—that the Order must go on, even if there was only one keeper left alive."

He looked up, eyes wet. "I have never told this to anyone, my friends. But this is Sarres, and now seems the time to make it known. Before I left him, Mardoc made me the next Archkeeper. He gave me the ring and prayed the words of Succession hastily over me while I kneeled in the muck, unworthy as I was. The Watch say the last Archkeeper is dead, but only I have known, all these years, that they are wrong. Because I am here. Solon the First."

There was utter silence.

Then Galen stood up. He went around the table; Solon rose to meet him. For a second they were still, until Galen kneeled, and Solon, hesitating, put his hands around the keeper's lifted hands, and said the words of Blessing;

strange, meaningless sounds to Carys, but to Raffi syllables of power.

And around the linked hands they saw it form, the Ring of the Archkeeper, one of the Order's most ancient relics, long thought lost. It was blue, fine as steel, and it rippled and ran as if it were a line of raw energy around the two men's wrists and fingers; even as they stared at it Solon's skin absorbed it again and it was gone, as if it had never been.

The Sekoi stood reverently.

Tallis had caught Raffi's hand and they kneeled too, and Carys stood up awkwardly, because she didn't know what else to do. She had rarely seen Galen so moved; for a long time he kept his head bowed as if unable to speak, and when he did his voice was raw with emotion.

"You should have told me." He looked up, his gaunt face keen with joy. "On the way here. You should have told me."

"I know." Solon lowered his hands. "Sit down, my friends. Please. Raffi, Tallis, please."

He seemed embarrassed. And yet the authority he claimed showed through; he was calm and could even smile now. "I can't say how relieved I am to have told someone. Such a secret is a great weight. But it must go no further, and must make no difference here. I was only chosen because there was no one else."

"You know the Makers act for a reason." Galen stood slowly, easing his stiff leg. "You are the rightful leader of the Order."

"Ah, but who knows how many are left?"

"How did you stay free?" Raffi blurted out. "How did you escape the Watch?" He was fascinated, Carys knew. His eyes shone as if he were hearing an old story come to life; she could feel the excitement in him.

Solon shook his head. "We left Mardoc. I'll never forget looking back from the hills and seeing the black figures of the Watchguard that surrounded that place. Nor how they dragged him out . . ." He glanced again at Flain's window, as if for help. "But he had outwitted them even at the end, and though he went to the torture, they say the Watch has never found the House of Trees. One old man defied them. I pray his sufferings were short."

The House of Trees. Carys wondered what he'd say when he knew they'd been there. That she'd been there.

In the stillness the fire crackled. A leaf-scutter rummaged in the beech tree outside the window. Felnia put her head around the door. "Marco's thirsty. Can I get him some ale?"

Tallis turned quickly. "Yes. Open a new flask. And Felnia!"

The little girl came back. "What?"

"Stop listening at the door."

Carys grinned. Felnia stuck her tongue out and vanished.

Solon looked nervous. "Will she tell Marco?"

"No. She's . . . been trained to keep secrets."

He nodded absently. "I must finish my story. I'll be brief. For years after Mardoc's death I eluded capture somehow. One of my scholars died—my dear Jeros, shot by a Watchpatrol as we fled through a town at night. We had to leave his body lying there in the dirt, without even a blessing. The other . . . he lost faith. He renounced the Makers. That was an even more bitter blow." He cleared his throat. "Finally, last year, I was caught, digging a relic up from some farmland. The farmer had his house burned and went to the mines. I was . . . interrogated."

He sat very still. Carys bit her lip and looked at Galen, who stood up and stalked to the window, looking out.

"Where did they take you?" she asked.

"A Watchtower."

"Number?"

"I'm not sure. Forty-five? At Feas Hill. A black, bitter place. I had no idea there were such places."

"What was the castellan's name?

"Timon. I think it was Timon."

Galen half turned and glared at her. She sat back.

"I don't know how long it lasted." Solon's long fingers rubbed the scars on his wrists; Carys knew he would have more, all over his body. "A stinking cell, endless beatings, torments. They have worms of Kest that devour flesh, burrow into the skin . . ."

His voice broke.

Tallis reached out and took his hand, and he smiled at her. After a moment he struggled on.

"All the brutality you have heard of the Watch, my children, all of it is true. I heard men tortured in other cells around me, screaming to die. And I was no hero. They broke me down soon enough. I would have told them anything they asked, because after a while there is only pain. The agony in your body fills all the world. I forgot the Order, but the Makers did not forget me. In one corner of my cell I scratched an image of Soren. No one else would have recognized it. In all the delirium and fear and darkness I sometimes thought she was there, speaking to me . . ."

Galen swung around. "And the Ring?"

"They never found that. As you know it cannot be seen or felt unless I wish it. I managed never to wish it."

"You were lucky," Carys said bluntly.

"I was. I knew so little that was of any use to them. I had seen no other keepers for years, knew no safe houses, no passwords, no networks of hiding places. In the end, I suppose they just grew tired of me. The Watch always have more prisoners to ill-treat. I was left alone for weeks. Then, one day, we were chained up and brought to Telman, to the Frost Fair, eleven of us. One died on the way. Marco and I were shackled together on the journey, the iron cutting into our legs. We became friends—unlikely friends, I admit, but then, we both fully expected to die, and I wanted to convert him. I thought I had accepted death. Until you came running up to me, Raffi, and the ice shattered. I still do not understand how that was done. But I thank Flain for his mercy." He smiled gently at Tallis, drawing his fingers back. "And you, Guardian, for your peaceful island."

She nodded, but from the window Galen said bleakly, "How much do you know about this Marco?" He turned, and they saw his face was dark. "Why were they holding him?"

"Ah." Solon looked awkward. His fingers stroked his neck as if he felt for awen-beads that had been long lost. "Yes. Marco. He's a good man, Galen. He tried to get free one night and they beat him with chains for it. He may not think quite like us, but . . ."

Galen came closer. He looked grim. "Archkeeper. What had he done?"

The older man smiled unhappily. "You won't like it."

"I can see that. Tell me."

Solon scratched his cheek. Then he said, "It appears Marco went back on a business deal with them. He cheated them. I'm afraid he is—was—a dealer, Galen. He sold relics to the Watch."

9

I have done dark things. Dark and terrible.
And I cannot undo them.

Sorrows of Kest

CARYS WINCED.

Galen exploded into rage. "He does *what*?"

"We must forgive him. He's a good man."

"A good man!" The keeper lashed a chair aside in fury. "Do you tell me we've brought such a man here! To Sarres! Half carried him for miles through wood and fen! Dear God, Solon, if I'd known, I'd have put the noose around his neck myself!"

"No, you wouldn't," the Archkeeper said mildly.

"You don't know me," Galen snarled. He strode across the room in wrath. "Men like that are the scum of the world. To steal the gifts of the Makers and sell

119

them for scrap! And you say he's your friend!"

"He is." Solon stood up. "Come, Galen. We are here to help the fallen, even those who have sunk so low they believe in nothing. He needs us. He may not know it, but he does."

Galen folded his arms, fighting for control. He took a deep breath, but when he spoke his voice was still acid with bitterness. "No wonder Mardoc chose you if you have kindness even for a wretch like this. I am not so perfect, Archkeeper."

"You've had a hard struggle. We all have." Solon came up to him hesitantly. "But he's here now. And for my sake, Galen, let him stay."

Galen looked at him in surprise. "You're the leader here, not me."

"I still ask you."

A shrill giggle interrupted them. They looked through the window and saw Marco limp painfully across the lawns, Felnia running in front of him. He sat carefully on a stone seat and gazed around, legs stretched out.

"For your sake," Galen said harshly. "But I pray he won't steal all of Sarres before the end."

"You blindfolded him," Carys pointed out.

He glared at her. "So I did."

"And now . . ." Solon sat down quickly, as if anxious to change the subject. "I have told my story, and someone, please, must tell me yours. I am eaten up with curiosity." He looked around the table at them contentedly. "I mean, how did you all come here? And if this is truly the island of Artelan's Dream, how is it uncorrupted? Above all"—he turned to look at Galen, who was still staring darkly out the window—"above all, keeper, how did you break the ice and speak to the trees with such strength? Because I have never seen the like of that in my life."

Galen did not turn. He seemed too morose to speak. "We came together in Tasceron," he said at last, heavy with irony.

"Tasceron!" Solon's eyes lit. "You've been there? There was a strange rumor going around the cells, that the Crow had risen over Tasceron. Is it true? Did you see it?"

Raffi and Carys looked at Galen, who turned slowly.

"No," he said.

The room went quiet. Carys saw at once that he wanted to keep the Crow a secret, and she thought he was wise.

But Raffi was trying to hide his astonishment, and even the Sekoi's yellow eyes widened a slit.

"We brought the girl here," Galen said.

Solon looked at Carys.

"Not me," she laughed. "Felnia."

"The little one? But why?"

"Because she is the Interrex." Galen came and sat down.

Solon stared. "The one spoken of in the Apocalypse? 'Between the kings the Interrex shall come'? But the Emperor is dead . . ."

"She's the Emperor's granddaughter," Raffi said quickly. He looked flurried; Carys wondered whether Galen had given him some mental signal to talk, to keep the conversation off the Crow.

"Are you sure?"

"Yes." Raffi rubbed his nose distractedly. "It's a long story. We found her in a Watchhouse." He explained, while Carys watched Galen. The keeper looked grim, his black hair pushed back. Through the window he watched Marco, sitting, eyes closed in the warm sun. It must hurt, Carys thought. Galen burned to tell Solon, to tell the world, that the Crow had returned, and yet it still wasn't safe. Though if it hadn't been for that man outside, Solon would know, she was sure.

Raffi finished his story and Solon stared in solemn astonishment. Finally he said, "So that little minx out there is the ruler of Anara! But yes . . ." Excitedly he turned to Galen. "That must be right! In the sixth chapter of the Apocalypse, Tamar implies that the Crow and the Interrex are somehow linked! They come together. I remember reading various commentaries on it for my studies—the Apocalypse is one of the more enigmatic books, as you know." He looked around. "My friends, this is a wonderful time we live in. Our next step is obvious. We have to find the Crow!"

Galen fingered the jet and green beads at his neck. He looked almost sick. He was about to speak when Tallis said calmly, "That may not be so. We have something to tell you that not even Galen knows."

Carys glanced at the Sekoi. It was biting its thumbnail, and smiled back at her archly.

Tallis turned to Galen. "While you've been away, we've made progress with the console."

"At last!"

"The console?" Solon murmured.

"A relic. Carys . . . brought it. From the Tower of Song."

Solon's eyebrows shot up. "How?"

"We'll explain later." Galen leaned across to Tallis, impatient. "What does it say? How much have you read?"

For answer she got up and crossed to a small chest of cedarwood that stood next to the hearth, and opened it. The fire had smoldered low; the Sekoi put some logs on, stirring up the blaze. Tallis came back.

Sitting down, she unwrapped a piece of black velvet and laid the console reverently on the smooth wood.

It was a small gray thing, made of Makers' material—not cold or warm, not metal or wood, a fabric unknown. Carys looked down at it, remembering the slimy stench of the worm she had fought off to get it. Small square buttons adorned it, each with a symbol. She had seen those many times in training, on relics studied in the Watchhouse, but not even the Order were sure what they meant anymore. Somewhere in the Tower of Song was the Gallery of Candlesticks, where thousands of clerks spent their lives making and breaking codes, but had never managed to decipher these.

Beside it Tallis laid some pieces of paper. Then she folded her fingers together and looked up.

"Galen and I had been trying to study this before he was called away. It is very ancient. I believe the memories inside it are those of one of the Makers themselves, perhaps Tamar, though he never gives his name. It has been difficult to read, because very little power is left in it. Raffi had to use most of it to escape from the Watchhouse, if you remember."

She touched the papers lightly. "But last week, on the day of Altimet, which I thought might be a good time, we tried again. Myself, and Carys, and our friend the Sekoi."

Galen looked surprised. Carys grinned at him.

"I needed stronger sense-lines than my own," Tallis explained. "Carys has much awen, though undirected, and Sekoi energies are powerful, even though they are strange to me. But we had to work in silence for over an hour before we made the entry."

"Did you use a Web or a Link?" Galen interrupted,

and Solon said, "Do the Sekoi have a third eye, then? I have never heard that."

Tallis smiled. "Keepers. The details can wait. Let's just say that we managed to insinuate our minds deep into the cracks and crevices of the device. There was a faint stirring of warmth there still, but so thin a whisper that I had to bring it out word by word, in some places letter by letter. Carys wrote the message down. Often we had to stop. It was exhausting."

"And very peculiar," the Sekoi muttered. It scratched its fur. "Small sparks like fleas crawled over my skull. And what a thirst I had afterward!"

"Without you we couldn't have done it," Tallis said. She swung the plait of hair over her shoulder and picked up the notes. Raffi could see they were untidy, with words crossed out and altered in Carys's regular Watch-script.

"Fragments of this you've heard before. This is the rest, as far as we could make out. It seems to have been recorded in a time of great crisis for the Makers."

She pushed an escaped lock of hair behind her ear, and began to read:

"Things are desperate; it may be that we will have to withdraw. There's been no word from Earth for months and we don't know how the Factions stand. Worst of all, we're sure now about Kest. Against all orders, he's tampered with the genetic material. Somehow he's made a hybrid. He never told us, but Soren guessed.

"The creature is hideous. Flain fears it has a disturbed nature, certainly a greatly enhanced lifespan. When it was let out of the chamber it destroyed all the lights and most of the test area. It seems to dislike light. Then it stood in the dark and spoke to Flain, taunting him. It is very intelligent.

"We have flung it deep in the Pits of Maar. Kest called it the Margrave. I hope it will die, but in my heart I keep thinking we should have destroyed it. We should have made sure."

Tallis stopped.

Solon had made a small gasp, an indrawing of breath. When they looked at him, his face was white with terror. Sudden cold tingled down Raffi's spine.

Galen leaned over. "Archkeeper? Are you ill?"

He shook his head, his fingers vaguely rubbing over

each other, as if he were washing his hands. "No. That name."

"The Margrave. You've heard it?"

"I have. In the cells."

He seemed frozen with dread. Raffi shivered too. A ripple of horror swept across the room like a snowstorm. All the sense-lines swirled, and for a moment Raffi saw again the darkness of his dream-vision; the dark room he had once seen, the edge of a misshapen face, long as a jackal's, turning toward him in the firelight. Then Galen said, "Raffi!" in an anxious snarl.

He opened his eyes.

Everyone seemed unsettled.

"No. My fault." Solon rubbed his forehead with the heels of his hands. "I must be more tired than I thought. Might I also have some ale, Guardian?"

Carys fetched it, thinking grimly that if even a word could unnerve them, it was no wonder the Order had crumbled so fast. Raffi came behind her and drank a deep draft from the cold water jug. His hands were clammy with sweat.

"All right?" she said.

"All right." He wiped his mouth.

"You remembered about the Margrave, didn't you? That time you saw it."

"I didn't see it. Not properly."

She nodded. He was taut and unwilling to talk. Together they carried the jug and cups back to the table.

Turning a page, Tallis read on:

"Kest's creatures swarm everywhere, multiplying and mutating. The geological patterns are uneven and yet the weather-net holds. When we withdraw we'll have to leave the Coronet active as a stabilizer, even if neural access is not possible. It should hold off the disintegration of the weather-net for decades, maybe centuries. Until we come back. Also, it may provide an emergency portal. Flain says . . ."

She stopped and looked up.

"Flain says?" Galen asked anxiously.

"I'm afraid that's all, keeper. Nothing else would come."

In the quiet the Sekoi picked up the jug and poured ale into the small wooden cups. Felnia came and looked around the door.

"I'm getting hungry. Haven't you finished YET?"

"Soon," Galen growled. "Keep him out there."

"Don't shout at me!" They heard her shooing the geese out of her way.

"They were in trouble," Carys said. "There were few of them, and Kest's interference had disrupted their creation of the world. They were in danger. So they left."

"Leaving us the Margrave," Raffi muttered.

"And Flain's Coronet," Galen said.

They all looked at him. His eyes were dark, his face tense with energy.

"Yes!" Solon nodded. "I had noticed that too."

"Is it a precious thing, this Coronet?" the Sekoi asked casually.

Tallis shrugged. "It's rarely mentioned in the sacred books. No one has ever thought it anything important. In images, Flain is sometimes shown as wearing a thin gold crown. As there."

The Sekoi's yellow eyes turned with interest to the window. Flain wore his dark robe of stars, and now they noticed on his hair a delicate filament of gold, smooth and without decoration. It was easy to miss, Carys thought.

"But it is important, obviously, and it's what we need." Galen stood up and walked across the room. "We must find it. All winter I've worried over this; we can't deal with the Margrave with the world crumbling around us. This may be the thing that will keep the Finished Lands safe . . ."

"But they're not safe," Raffi muttered. "They're shrinking."

"Exactly!" Galen turned on him, dark hair swinging out of its knot of string. "And this relic might stop that! We have to find out where it is!"

"And the Margrave?" Carys asked.

"Can't know about that. The Margrave is the secret power behind the Watch. If they knew, then the Watch would be looking for the Coronet. Unless . . ." He sat down suddenly. "Unless this is what the Watch are really seeking, when they confiscate relics."

They thought for a moment. Then the Sekoi said, "And how do we even know where to look?"

"We ask." Galen turned to Tallis, the air around him almost crackling with his conviction. "We use Artelan's Well. One of us drinks the water, and this time"—he glared at Raffi—"there'll be no mistakes."

"Sorry to interrupt," a voice said wryly from the door, "but have you people finished your service? It's just that the little one and I could eat skeats."

Galen straightened and stared at him. "You."

Marco stared back. Then he looked ruefully at Solon.

"Thanks, Your Holiness. I see you've told our hosts all about me."

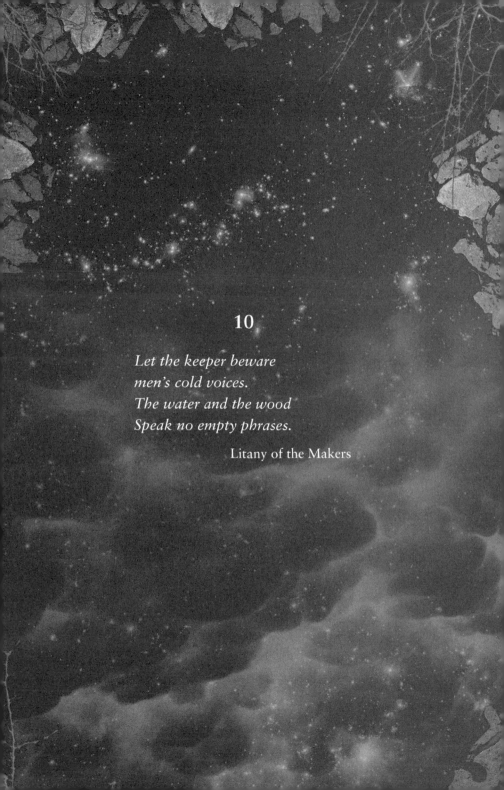

10

Let the keeper beware
men's cold voices.
The water and the wood
Speak no empty phrases.

Litany of the Makers

RAFFI STOOD ON THE HILL, the sky above him a clear, warm blue. He could see the small red moon, Pyra, the youngest of the sisters and his favorite, very pale in the sunlight. Looking up at her, quite suddenly he remembered one time when he had been small, sitting on his mother's lap, hearing the story of Pyra and the wolf, while his brothers and sisters ran and argued around him. When could that have been? His mother had always been too busy to pay much attention to him. How were they all? he wondered. It had been a long time since he had thought about home, though it had always been there, a place to go back to in the corner of his mind. He knew it had been dirty, noisy, full of arguments; he'd always been in the way, under people's feet, a dreamer. He probably wouldn't like it if he went back, he thought sadly, looking out. In a way, Sarres was home now.

All the green island lay beneath him, its orchards barely breaking into blossom, its lanes and hedges, where already the white snowcaps and muskwort were out, and banks of yellow crocus sprouted from the rich soil. In Sarres spring came early, the ground ripe with Maker-power, and all over it, in the hush when the breeze dropped, you could hear the endless, invisible trickle of Artelan's Well, the spring of water that ran clear as crystal, that Flain had promised would never dry up.

Raffi let his mind slide deep in the energy lines of the island, sending small sense-filaments into branch and root, into worms and birds and water, feeling the green, fresh restlessness, the small pains of awakening.

A sound brought him out abruptly; the soft whirr and thwack of a crossbow bolt. He opened his eyes, sense-lines swirling, then ran, slipping in haste down the steep, wet grass. Halfway down the sound came again, closer, but in complete silence. No one called or yelled.

He slowed, sweating, letting the panic go. Stupid. There were no Watch on Sarres.

Or rather, just the one.

Ducking under the trees he came through the small iron gate onto the lawns and saw Carys. She had set up a circle of wood on a rickety open ladder and was aiming at it, standing well back. As he watched, her finger tightened on the trigger; from here he could see her one eye close, feel the strain of concentration swell inside her like a bright bubble. Then it burst, instantly, and the bolt thumped into the wood.

Carys bent and picked another out of the grass. She looked over.

"What are you doing?" he asked.

She slotted the bolt in. "Stupid question. You can see."

"Yes, but I mean why?"

"To keep my hand in." She tucked the smooth hair behind one ear. "And to be ready for when we go."

"We're not going till after the Feast," he said, his heart cold. "And Carys, you can't come!"

She grinned at him. "Oh can't I?"

"Your picture was on that death-list!"

To his surprise she just laughed. "Of course it was! Don't worry, Raffi. I can cut my hair and change its color. They taught us all about that."

"You can't change your face."

"You'd be surprised how bad people's memories are. I'll take my chance." She wound the bolt back rapidly.

He wandered over, knowing it was useless to argue. "You'd be safe here."

"I'm coming. If Galen's going after this Coronet, then so am I." She aimed deliberately. Watching, he felt the weight of the bow in his mind; then he opened his third eye and from the target saw the bolt explode into his chest with a wooden thump.

"I've been thinking," he said. "Why weren't we on that list? Galen and me?"

"They don't have drawings of you."

"Braylwin would have described us. They could have made some sort of picture."

She looked at him, thinking. "There are lots of lists. Still, you're right. It's odd."

A mere-duck flew over, its red tail flashing. She whipped up the bow, following it down among the trees.

"Don't," he muttered, nervous.

Carys looked at him irritably. "It's not loaded."

"I'm very glad of that!" Marco was walking through the trees. In the last few days his wounds had almost healed; looking at him now Raffi saw a stocky, broad-shouldered man in the too-tight red jerkin Tallis had found for him. Red of face too, a bold, blunt, cheery face. He sat himself down next to them.

"Now, I'd love to know why a scholar of the Order needs to practice with a crossbow. Maybe if I wasn't a hated relic-dealer, and in Galen's opinion lower than the muck on his boot, I'd ask."

Raffi frowned. Carys laughed. Lowering the bow she kneeled on the grass. "I'm not a scholar. I'm ex-Watch. A bit like you, I suppose."

"Ex-Watch!" Marco looked curious. "I didn't think they allowed any 'ex.'"

She shrugged.

After a silence he said, "My friend Solon tells me we'll only be here three more days. Until after the Feast of the Field of Gold. Whatever that is."

Raffi looked appalled. "You don't know?"

Marco lay back on one elbow, ankles crossed. "Should I?" he teased.

"It's Flain's return. From the Underworld. From the dead."

"Oh." Marco winked at Carys. "I see. From the *dead*!"

Raffi felt himself going red. The man was making fun of him. And the Makers. It made him angry. "It's important," he muttered fiercely. "It's the first day of spring."

"I'm sure it is. Where would we be without the Makers."

Raffi scrambled up.

"Wait. I'm sorry." Marco sat upright, his grin suddenly gone. "Really, Raffi. I shouldn't poke fun at you. Not after you all but took my head out of the noose. It's just . . ." He shook his head in irritation. "How an intelligent man like Solon can believe all that nonsense . . ."

"Is it though?" Carys said thoughtfully. "How would you explain the world, Marco? Relics—you must have handled a lot of those. And Sarres?"

He pulled a mock painful face and rubbed an eyebrow;

he had thick eyebrows, as if his hair had been dark, and across his knuckles the word ROSE tattooed in blue. "I'm a plain man, Carys. How should I know. There were Makers—there probably were—but I think they were people just like us. Well, cleverer. Where they came from, I don't know, but I don't believe they came down from the stars on stairs of silver! They knew things we don't; the relics were things they made. Over the centuries the Order built up these fancy stories about them and forgot all the important bits. And why not? It gave them plenty of power. Men like Solon would have been respected. Before the Watch."

She glanced over at Raffi. He looked hot and confused.

"And the power the keepers have? It exists. I've seen it."

"So have I!" Marco laughed. "Oh, I can't explain that. The ice-cracking was incredible, but when Galen got those trees to close in around us—that would have made my hair stand on end if I still had any!"

They laughed with him, Raffi uncomfortably.

"It comes from the Makers, I suppose. It still doesn't make them gods."

"They weren't gods," Raffi muttered. "They were the sons of God."

Marco lay back in the grass, hands behind his head. "Whatever," he said lazily.

IT SCARED RAFFI. He couldn't talk to Galen about it because for two days the keeper had been deep in the rituals of preparation—fasting, meditating alone, on the hill and by the spring. And anyway, Raffi knew Galen too well. He'd have laughed harshly, and given him some chapters of the Book to study. Or told him off for listening to unbelievers.

Sitting in the dark, silent room that night, with the fire and all the candles out, in the cold stillness before the day of the Return, Raffi found himself wondering about the Makers. Flain and Tamar, Soren, Halen, Theriss, Kest. All his life he had known of them, had spoken to them. Often he felt they were close to him, answering when he needed them. Sometimes there was just silence. He knew all the stories, had even stood in the House of Trees itself. And there he had heard a voice, a living voice, full of distance. A voice from beyond the stars.

Marco couldn't explain that away, could he?

Raffi shifted. He was stiff and cold and almost light-headed with hunger after fasting all day. Next to him Solon turned for a moment and smiled. It made Raffi feel better. He and Galen, Solon and Tallis sat silent. Even sense-lines were forbidden now, in the darkest time before dawn. All night since sundown they had waited, without food, without light, without speech. As Flain had done. Because this was what it must be to be dead.

With a creak, the door opened.

Carys put her head around and slipped in. After her came the Sekoi, a tall, thin shadow, carrying Felnia, looking tousled and half asleep, still clutching her worn toy, Cub.

At the back, Marco followed. The bald man closed the door silently and leaned against it, folding his arms. Seeing Raffi's stare, he grinned.

Tallis stood up, stiff. Tonight she was an old woman, and wore a dark crimson dress.

"Keepers," she said. "The night ends. The time has come."

All the doors and windows were opened. Outside, the

darkness was absolutely still, the sky mottled with high, pale clouds, moon-edged. Agramon and Cyrax were full, and Lar's pitted face a ghostly shadow.

It was Solon who led them out, stiff with sitting, over the gray lawns in the night-chill and up the hill, climbing the long slope silently to the top, and as they stood there in a breathless line the wind gusted, lifted Carys's hair and Galen's coat. Felnia had gone back to sleep; the Sekoi propped her against its thin shoulder.

They waited, seeing all the darkness of Sarres below them, until Solon began the Canticle of Flain, his voice strange, as if someone else spoke through him.

I, who had been in the dark, am come into the light.

From the bitter places of the Underworld I bring all I have learned.

For without pain how can there be joy?

And without darkness how can there be light?

Without hatred how can there be love?

How can there be life without the selflessness of death?

He raised his hands. A few birds had begun to sing in the woods; the sky in the east was pale, the underside of the clouds lit with a red glow.

Mardoc's Ring

There is no darkness black enough to swallow me.

There is no chasm deep enough to bury me.

There is no fear cold enough to empty me.

My heart is full; my heart holds all the world.

The sky brightened. All the woods and fields were alive with birdsong. On the tip of the horizon far in front of them, among the mists and fog of the marshes, a slit of scarlet slashed the gray. Herons flew over, three in a row. All the keepers were chanting now, and Raffi with them, hands out.

Behold, Anara, I have returned to you from the Pit,

Bringing daylight,

Bringing the spring.

I have been dead. I have been alive.

In all the hollows of your heart there is nowhere that I have not been.

And at last the sun burned before them, vivid as fire, catching Galen's face and Carys's, and the Sekoi's grin and Felnia's yawn and Solon's outstretched hands. It shone in Tallis's flame-red hair and she laughed; it stung Raffi's eyes to wetness and Marco's broad face to a tolerant smile.

All around them, Sarres was a Field of Gold.

11

Pyra looked up at the hot eyes of the Wolf. "I'm not scared of you," she said.

"Indeed?" the Wolf said politely, coming a step closer.

"No. Because I come from the sky."

"You don't say!" The Wolf came closer still.

The wind rippled her red cloak. "I could singe your fur," she warned.

The Wolf grinned, showing sharp teeth. "Go on then," he muttered.

Pyra and the Wolf

"**H**OW LONG, SMALL KEEPER?" the Sekoi asked anxiously.

Raffi yawned. "Ten hours, nearly."

The room was black, lit only with two guttering candles and the dull ashes of the fire. It was the second night since the Feast, and Galen was deep in the dream-coma.

The others took turns to come and go, but Raffi had to stay. It was part of his duty as Galen's scholar—though even without that, he knew he could never have settled to anything else.

The keeper lay on a couch near the fire, to keep

him warm. He lay still, without a flicker of movement, the sullen light making strange quivers over his face, his long hair. He was far, far away. Reaching out now, Raffi's sense-lines could find no trace of him, only a great vacancy like a black pit, so that Raffi had to pull back from its edge, cold fear churning his stomach. It had happened before. In every meditation Galen walked far. But Raffi could never get used to that emptiness.

He was tired, though he'd slept a few hours, curled in the corner while Carys and Tallis kept watch. Now, with the Sekoi here, he felt a bit more wakeful.

"If I drank this well-water," the creature mused, propping its spindly legs up on a chair, "would this happen to me?"

Raffi shrugged. "It did when I drank it."

"I remember! What a panic we were in! But you have had some training."

"Not much. I'm on the fourth branch."

"And that isn't high?" the Sekoi asked politely.

"No." Raffi prowled over and put a log on the fire. "Not really."

"We've been too busy for you to be learning much, maybe. And now"—it looked at him slyly out of one eye—"now we have to travel again."

"Yes." Raffi sat down, staring at the sizzling log. He felt gloom creep over him.

The Sekoi nodded smugly, as if Raffi had confirmed something. "You want to stay," it said.

Raffi didn't deny it. He didn't say anything. All his mind was full of the last two days: the Feast with its tables of food, the warm comfortable rooms, the small, silly presents everyone had made for each other. Felnia dancing with Marco to the small viola that Tallis played, the Sekoi singing one of its endless tuneless songs with a chorus that convulsed Carys into hysterics.

In Sarres everything was clean, warm, ordered; everything was as it should be. There were set times for lessons and reading and work and just playing around. The Litany was said properly; all the feasts and fasts he had half forgotten were remembered. Above all there was no Watch, no fear, no constant staying alert, moving on. But it was a failing of his, this wanting to hide, to be safe. Galen had warned him about it. They were never out of the hands of the Makers if they did the work of the Order. Wherever it led them.

Galen's hand twitched.

Instantly the Sekoi was bending over him, Raffi hovering anxiously. The keeper's hand clenched, as if he gripped something invisible. Behind them, Solon came in and said in a quiet voice, "If he doesn't come out by morning, Tallis and I will go in for him."

"His breathing's changed." The Sekoi spread its long hands over Galen's chest and looked up. "I think he's waking."

The sense-lines were coming back. Raffi could feel them, flooding the dark room with a charge of energy, surging from somewhere incredibly remote.

Solon came quickly, feeling Galen's pulse. He gave a sidelong look at Raffi and said, "Your master has a strange energy. I can feel it swooping into him like a great darkness. As if something wilder than himself lived in him." He smiled, puzzled.

Raffi looked down.

"He never did tell me," the Archkeeper said gently, "how he broke the ice. Will you tell me, Raffi?"

"Ask him yourself," the Sekoi muttered, to Raffi's relief. "He's awake."

Galen's eyes opened. For a second he seemed to stare at nothing, but then his gaze focused and he pushed himself up on one hand stiffly.

"How long?" he croaked.

"Ten hours." Raffi had water ready; he poured a cupful and Galen drank thirstily, all their eyes intent on him.

"Well?" Solon asked eagerly. "Did you learn anything? Did the Makers speak to you?"

The keeper glanced up, his hooked face shadowed with weary hollows. Echoes and taints of strange images flowed from him, a crackle of light around his hands that made Solon stare.

"Oh yes," he whispered.

"AT FIRST THERE WAS JUST CONFUSION." Galen sat against the calarna tree in the morning sun and looked around the circle. They were all there, even Marco, who had drifted over and lounged in the shade. Galen ignored him.

"The Ride," Tallis observed. Today she was a small girl; she and Felnia were making a huge daisy chain, working one at each end.

"The Ride, yes. As soon as I had controlled that, I began to direct the dream. I spoke to Flain and asked him about the Coronet, to show me where it was and whether it was our duty to find it. When I had finished, I looked down and saw Anara."

"The whole planet?" Solon asked, surprised.

"Yes. I was high above it, among the moons and stars. Below me I could see the vast expanse of the sea, and the Finished Lands were green and healthy, but so small, Archkeeper, so tiny from that height! And as the planet turned I saw the Unfinished Lands, over half the globe and spreading; a terrible, churning destruction, a world burning and dissolving and erupting into chaos.

"The sight filled me with a sort of horror, but then someone called my name, and I turned. There were the moons, all seven of them, making the Arch behind me; Atelgar and Lar, Cyrax, Pyra, Agramon, Karnos, and Atterix, and I seemed to be drifting just above their surfaces. How different they all are!" He frowned, remembering.

"Agramon is smooth and white. There is nothing on it at all, no hills or valleys, its surface is as smooth as a ball, and yet there are ruined buildings there, and a thing that looks like a broken dome. And Pyra burns, her face is ravaged. Smoke comes in great plumes from explosions deep within her."

"This is an amazing vision," Solon muttered.

"It gets stranger." Galen scratched his hair. "It would take too long to tell you all I saw of the moons, but after an endless time I found a silver staircase and walked down it; a long, long descent until I was in a place full of animals. A jungle."

He frowned. "There were creatures there I had never imagined. And I was inside them. First I was a night-cat, then a long winding vesp, then a wasp. I changed into hundreds of shapes, slithering from one to another; I lost count, lost all sense of myself. The colors and scents bewildered me—did you know, Solon, that a hammerbird sees only blue, everything blue, while a grendel's eyes fracture light into a million colors we have no names for and can't even dream? It was exhilarating and terrifying. I grew wings and fur and beaks and tails, I was huge and

then tiny, shifting between shapes until my whole body
ached for it to stop but it just went on, the creatures more
warped now, with spines, too many eyes, deformed legs
and minds. I became all the deliberate horrors Kest has
made, seeing through their eyes, feeling their agony. I was
broken and evil, full of hate. I was blind and unfeeling.
My veins burned with poisons."

Felnia stared at him, fascinated, the daisy chain forgotten in the grass.

Galen paused. When he went on, his voice was harsh,
rigorously controlled. "Finally, all in an instant, I became
something brimming with intelligence. I thought I was
back to myself and looked at my hands, but they were
misshapen, with bent nails, and they were holding a mirror, so I raised it and looked in. I saw . . . a face. Beyond
the darkest of nightmares. Long, reptilian, yet with a
snout like a jackal's, or a tomb-dog's, and eyes that were
so evil I had to close them, because I feared for my soul
if I looked into them. And then the laughter came, and it
wasn't me that was laughing but the Margrave, and yet I
was inside the laughter, I was trapped in it and couldn't
get out."

He stopped.

In the silence a bird sang carelessly just above them. Small fleecy clouds crossed the sky.

Galen's whole body was tense. Slowly he relaxed; his palms were wet with sweat.

Solon was pale. "Everywhere we turn," he whispered, "we meet this creature."

"And you saw him?" Carys asked.

"Clearly." Galen half glanced at Marco, then rubbed his face with his hands and went on grimly. "Everything went dark. I wandered in confusion after that. The vision was broken for hours, years, it seemed. I began to think I would never get out. Until I saw a small yellow flower, lying on the ground."

"Flainscrown!" Raffi sat up.

"Yes." Galen's eyes lit. "As soon as I saw it, I knew I was myself. I picked it up, and beyond it there was another, and then another. I followed them."

"Like the story of the children in the wood," Felnia put in gravely.

They all laughed, breaking the tension. Galen reached over and pushed her into the grass. "Like that, yes." He looked at Carys. "Someone had been strewing them, so I followed, and walked out of the darkness into a green field. There in front of me were seven girls wearing yellow dresses. Each had a basket; they were spreading the flowers on the ground in a great circle. I walked up to them, and knew who they were."

"The seven sisters," Carys muttered.

"Exactly. Atelgar, Lar, Cyrax, all of them. Pyra was the youngest, Agramon the eldest. They stood around me in a ring on the grass and they walked, Carys, all around me, laughing and saying, 'Look at us, keeper. Look at us!' until I was dizzy and sick with it and all I seemed to see was light, seven flickers of falling light getting so close, they were burning me. I reached out and pushed one away. And then . . ." He shrugged, shaking his head. "Then I woke up."

There was silence. Into it Marco said drily, "I must try some of that well-water myself!"

Galen glared at him in sudden cold fury, but Solon was nodding. "Fascinating! 'Look at us.' That was what they said. Do you notice how you saw the moons twice? Once as worlds, as they are, and once as the sisters, as they appear in tales. They were also strewing the flowers. To lead you to them."

Marco grinned, but Solon looked at him sharply. "Don't mock us, old friend."

"Sorry," the bald man said, "but I fail to see how you can get to—"

"Not get to them. Look at them. There is a place where we can do that. About twenty miles east of Tasceron."

"The observatory!" Carys said suddenly.

Tallis nodded. "So I have been thinking."

"What's that?" Felnia asked bluntly, and Raffi was glad because he didn't know either.

"It's a tower," Carys said. "The Order used to use it for observing the moons. There were relics there—it was one of the sites we studied on the Relic Recognition course."

"I'm glad you know so much about it," Solon said mildly. "You must give us that course someday. But it would be the obvious place to start looking. There were once detailed plans of the moons there. Nothing may remain. But it seems clear the Makers wish us to link the Coronet with the moons in some way."

"I suppose so." Galen looked at Tallis, who threaded a last daisy and nodded.

"Yes. Though I wish the Margrave had not appeared in your vision." She glanced at Raffi. "That disturbs me."

The Sekoi folded its long fingers, thoughtful.

"I only wish," Solon said impulsively, "that you had had some message about the Crow!"

Galen stood up. He looked down at Marco darkly.

"Maybe the Crow will make himself known on the way."

The Vortex

12

Kest armed himself against the Dragon, but Flain caught his arm. "There is no need for this," he said.

Kest shook his head. "There is every need. I created this—evil; I must prove to you that I can destroy it. And if I die, I will die in peace."

Book of the Seven Moons

RAFFI CROUCHED IN THE BEECH WOOD, looking down. Far below, deep in the valley, the road was invisible, but he could see the bridge.

Galen had the relic-glass open and was looking through it. "Double gates. Dogs. Guard post at each end," he said grimly.

A Watchman came out of one of the small buildings, paced slowly over the bridge and into the other. Nothing else moved.

Galen snapped up the tube.

"May I look at that?" Marco sounded fascinated.

Galen glared at him. Then, to Raffi's surprise, he

handed the relic over, watching as the man fingered it. Marco whistled in envy. "This would make a thousand, maybe two, on the market."

Behind them Solon sighed from his seat on the beech roots. "I don't know which of you is crueler to the other," he said severely.

Galen said nothing.

Marco gave the relic back; the keeper's hand closed over it tightly.

A crackle of twigs made them turn, alert, but Raffi had already sensed Carys and the Sekoi coming back, climbing carefully up the slippery, crumbling bank, ankle-deep in fallen leaves.

Carys had cut her hair very short and dyed it red. As she clambered over the top and stood, hands on hips, getting her breath, she looked strange, like someone new. "There's a place upstream," she gasped. "Some rocks. It looks shallow enough, but fast."

The Sekoi sat down, disgusted. "I hate water," it muttered.

Galen looked at Solon. "I don't think we have any choice. The bridge will be too difficult. Will you manage?"

The Vortex

Solon gave a gracious smile. "My son, I've waded many rivers in my time. With Flain's help I'll manage one more."

"Then lead on, Carys. If you're sure."

She didn't move. "I'm not. You'll need to tell me what you think."

"Why?" Marco asked.

"It's too obviously a good place to cross. They must know about it. I would think there'll be pits out in the river, or underwater nets." She frowned. "There must be something."

Galen looked at her. "Let's go down," he said at last. "We may be able to tell."

The path was rocky, winding between birches and beeches and firethorns, a slippery, treacherous trail they had been following for days through the high woods. It was an outlaw-road, used only by thieves and keepers and, Raffi suspected, the Sekoi, on their mysterious journeys. Now they left it and plunged down the slope. Raffi let his sense-lines ripple out through the empty wood, feeling the dim gathering of winter twilight, the cold, curled hibernation of hedgehogs and small furred rootvoles deep in their hollows under the leaves. Far to the east a rosy glow still lit distant cliffs, but as they descended into the valley, the sun faded out, the short afternoon already darkening. Slithering down the slope Raffi allowed himself one brief memory of the warmth of Sarres.

They had left the island five days ago, Tallis and Felnia standing hand in hand on the lawns watching them go, the Guardian tall and young, her long hair in its thick braid. Felnia had wanted to come, and she'd stormed and scowled at them until they were almost lost in the mist. Then, just as Raffi had stepped onto the wicker causeway, she'd wailed his name and he'd turned.

"This time," she'd hissed, "get me that present!"

But the fog had closed in and Sarres was gone.

Since then, they had plunged back into winter. At first Raffi had thought he was the only one worried by the cold, but over the last day or so he'd become aware of Galen's growing unease. The spring was far too late. On the beech trees now, as he slid among their smooth roots, all the black buds were tightly furled. No birds sang. For the last two nights the frost had been bitter. Small bulbs were barely poking through the leaf-drift. And something felt wrong. Like a clock with a tick slightly lagging, a melody that dragged half a note behind.

Galen knew. So, Raffi guessed, did Solon, but none of them had spoken of it yet.

Missing his footing, Raffi slid abruptly and sat down hard, the Sekoi glancing back and laughing at him. They worked their way slowly along the treacherous bank, Solon leaning on the trees and easing himself down.

Near the bottom, Carys was waiting.

When they caught up, she led them along a narrow path cautiously.

"It's all right," Raffi said. "There's no one around."

She glared back at him. "I've never understood how you know that."

"Sense-lines. It's easier with three of us." For a moment he thought of the dark days of Galen's accident and shivered.

"But what are they?"

"Feelings. Strings of them. Like the ripples in a pool."

She made a snorting sound. "You'll have to teach me."

"I can't. You're not in the Order. Besides, only some people can do it."

She grinned over her shoulder. "I could do it."

"Yes. I'll bet you could."

"Bet?" The Sekoi's voice was sly in his ear. "How much?"

But Carys had stopped. "This is it, Galen."

Below, the path sloped to a shingly spit. The river, called the Wyren, ran fast here, its brown water rippling into white foam against the rocks. They had to cross it, but both bridges so far had been well guarded, and the river didn't seem to be getting any narrower.

Looking over, Raffi saw holly and scrubby low bushes on the far bank. There seemed to be some sort of muddy foreshore there too. In the middle of the stream a few large rocks jutted. A bird was perched on one, a heavy mud-colored creature with a huge horny beak. It flew off with a troubled, mournful cry when it saw them.

Nothing else moved.

Galen's glance traveled across the brown, rippling water. Raffi knew how difficult this was; his own sense-lines had easily been swirled away by the rapid energies of the river.

At last the keeper said, "There's nothing of the Watch here."

The Vortex

"You think." Marco looked doubtful. He climbed down the bank and crouched on the shingle, fingering long grooves in it. "Something fairly big was dragged up here not long ago."

"Yes, but Galen is right." Solon eased himself down and took off his long gray coat with a shiver. "There is nothing unnatural, as there would be if the river was staked or netted. It seems as good a place as any."

He crouched and began to wash his hands in the stream, rubbing away green lichen from the trees. Galen watched him; Solon glanced up.

"My son? Do you want to try elsewhere?"

"No." The keeper limped down to join him. "We haven't time. It will be dark in an hour."

He was right, but they all felt a little uneasy. The place was too silent, and the roaring of the icy water chilled them. The Sekoi took some rope from its pack and tied one end firmly to a beech trunk. Then it turned, reluctant.

"Who goes first?"

"I do." Galen and Marco said it together, and their eyes met. "Because," Marco went on calmly, "I was once a sailor and have swum wilder seas than this. Also, I don't have a stiff leg that bothers me. Thanks to Sarres I'm as fit as I've ever been."

Galen looked at him coldly but didn't argue. The Sekoi handed the rope over; Marco tied it around his broad chest and waded in.

"Be careful," Solon said anxiously.

"Old friend, I fully intend to be."

It must have been freezing, but he was strong, and at first the water was shallow. About five paces out he staggered slightly, and then was suddenly up to his chest, the roaring current foaming under his lifted arms. The Sekoi let the rope out, so that it dipped in the water and whipped up taut, flinging off drops like tiny crystals.

The river raged. Glints and whirls of it slid through Raffi's skull. A flash of phosphorescence, green as glass.

Marco struggled on. He was nearly at the rocks now, but the current dragged mercilessly at him, so that he jerked sideways. The Sekoi wound the rope around its thin wrists, heaving back; Galen grabbed on too.

Marco called something, words lost in the water-roar. His hand came up and pointed, dripping.

"What?" Carys shouted.

The Vortex

Another flicker. Raffi felt it shoot toward him, green and evil, saw its speed, its savagery, the gleaming intricate scales of its back.

"Galen!" he breathed.

But the keeper already had the rope tight. "Pull him back!" he yelled at the Sekoi. "Get him back! *Now*!"

Marco fell. Around him the water churned; he slipped and all at once was gone, his head bobbing up yards downstream, the rope unraveling with whiplash speed. Raffi grabbed it; the heat of the slithering coils burned through his gloves.

"My God!" Solon gasped. "What is that?"

As they hauled desperately at the rope, something was sliding up through the torrent beyond the rocks; a long crooked snout, a spiny crest, three eyes just above the surface, dark and narrow. Marco took one look and turned, kicking furiously for the shore. The current tore at him. Galen heaved on the rope.

"Carys!" he thundered.

"Got it." She had the bow aimed; almost at once she fired, and the bolt sliced the water just past Marco's head. He gave a howl of terror. The river roared and chasmed.

And out of it rose a creature that made the hairs on Raffi's arms and neck prickle with pure dread; a nightmare of Kest's, its body scaled and ridged, mossed with tangled weeds that clung to it, encrusted with growths and hideous scrambling crabs. Carys's bolt had struck it in the throat; it was gagging and choking, slime and blood hanging in spumes from wide jaws, behind it the whole river thrashing and raging in fury.

The rope was halfway in, wet and icy. Carys jammed another bolt in, swearing savagely.

The creature crashed down.

For a second the world was water, soaking them all. Marco's face was a screech somewhere, seared with fear. "Pull him!" Galen drove his feet in, the rope taut. They were all heaving now, Raffi's muscles cracking and aching with the weight.

The river opened huge jaws. Water foamed; there was blood in it. Marco was yelling, and the second bolt thumped into the scaled loops around him with a scream that might have been anyone's; then in the river's convulsions he was suddenly crumpled there, on the shingle, gasping, with Solon standing over him.

The Vortex

The Archkeeper kneeled and grabbed Marco's arm. "Are you alive?"

The bald man managed a nod, and Solon stared up. "Back, creature of evil!" he shouted.

It hung above them, bending over them both like a wave. And then it slithered and streamed back and dissolved; the river gave up one great bubble, and ran smooth.

13

Surveillance reports must be studied.
Information must be collated and acted
on. Failure to do so is a punishable
offense.

Rule of the Watch

FOR A LONG TIME THEY SAT SILENT under the trees, cold and utterly dispirited. The sun had gone; now twilight gathered, smelling of damp fungi. Marco still shivered, despite his borrowed layers of dry clothes.

They were all thinking the same thing, but it was Carys who said it. "No wonder they didn't need to guard the crossing."

"Was that an avanc?" the Sekoi wondered. "Never have I heard of one so far inland."

"If it was, the spines are new," Galen growled. He glanced at Marco. "And the stench."

They could still smell it, a putrid fishy reek that brought clouds of gnats and hungry bloodflies out of the dark undergrowth. Solon slapped one off his face. "This is not a healthy place to mope, my friends."

Carys sat up. "Quite right. So here's what we do."

"If you think," Marco said savagely, "that I'm going anywhere near—"

"Save your breath. And forget the river. We're going over the bridge."

They all stared at her. Then Galen said, "Go on."

She put her fingers together. "For a start, there'll be no more than four Watchmen on a crossing this remote. We'll need to split them up—a diversion. You can do that, Galen. Also, there'll be dogs . . ."

"We can deal with most dogs," Galen said briefly.

She nodded. "Right. Say we get them here in the wood. The other two men will stay on the bridge."

"Which is double-barred," the Sekoi murmured.

"Which is double-barred. So we get them to open it."

Solon looked at her as if all this was too fast for him. "How?"

"A traveler wants to cross. Someone on his own. Not

a keeper. Not on any wanted list. Someone they don't know. Unarmed. Harmless."

There was an uneasy silence.

The Sekoi looked up and saw everyone was looking at it. "Great," it said acidly. It scratched its tribemark and managed a sour smile. "Kind of you to think of me, Carys."

"You've done worse."

"Oh? And what do you suggest I say to them when I get through the gate? With a crossbow pointed at each eye?"

Carys smiled sweetly. "I think you should tell them a story."

THE TWO WATCHMEN STOOD in silence on the bridge.

"Can you still see them?"

"The lanterns. Just there."

Between the trees small yellow lights flickered.

"What do you think it was?"

The taller man shrugged. "The avanc. You can smell it. It's had some riverfox or other."

Far off, the dogs barked. Deep in the woods the lanterns were lost for a moment, and a gray owl hooted. Under the roar of the water the silence was oppressive. Then a whistle blew. Six short blasts; one long.

Both men relaxed. The signal meant: "Investigating further. No danger."

"Riverfox," the smaller man said, turning away. "Nothing else screams like that."

"RIGHT." CARYS DROPPED THE WHISTLE into her pocket. "Off you go."

The Sekoi glared at her, then at the two Watchmen crumpled in the shadows, their dogs curled up contentedly beside them. Raffi helped it on with its pack, the creature plucking the straps into place with its long fingers. It looked nervous and lanky.

"We'll be right outside," Raffi said.

"Small keeper, I'd be happier if you were inside."

Galen stood up. "If you don't want to . . ."

"Of course I don't want to." The Sekoi's voice was an exasperated snarl. "However, I'll go. The logic of the choice was impeccable. It's just . . ." Its yellow eyes flickered to Carys. "I just wish someone else had suggested it."

She tucked her red hair behind one ear and grinned.

Quietly, they all moved through the wood. On the edge of the trees the Sekoi stopped, put its hand into its coat, and made odd wriggling movements. Then it dumped a warm money belt into Raffi's hands.

"A few small coins for the Great Hoard. If I don't come back, pass them on to any Sekoi."

Raffi felt the weight of it in amazement. "You've been busy."

The Sekoi winked.

Then it was loping up the track to the bridge. Dappled moonlight lit its back, sending three tall shadows into the trees.

"A brave soul," Solon muttered, half to himself. Behind him, Galen nodded.

When the creature got to the bridge it looked back, once. Through the sense-lines Raffi felt nothing, but the Sekoi were notoriously hard to reach. It turned and pulled a long cord.

Somewhere a bell jangled.

Crouching beside Solon under a fallen tree thick with ivy, Raffi felt rather than saw the Watchman who opened the grille. They were too far to hear what was said, but the words "Another one" rang in the sense-lines for a moment, and he knew the man had been sour, but hardly surprised.

He glanced at Solon. "They were expecting him?"

The Archkeeper looked grave. "They were expecting someone, my son. I pray we haven't made a great mistake."

The gate was opening. Like a shadow the Sekoi slipped in. The bolts shot to behind it, then the inner gate was opened; Raffi felt the slow, heavy drag of the wood, deep in the curved groove it had worn in the floor.

It slammed in his head.

And the river swirled by, breaking the sense-lines.

Galen leaned his head back against the ivy-covered tree.

"Now we wait," he muttered.

186

The Vortex

IT SHOULDN'T HAVE TAKEN THIS LONG. Restless, Raffi strapped the belt of coins tighter under his shirt. It felt strangely heavy, as if it weighed him down. Keepers had no money—that was one of the Precepts of the Order. Idly he wondered what it would be like to spend all this.

After a daydream of warm beds and fine food, he came back to himself to find Solon praying the Litany quietly and Carys talking to Marco, lying on one elbow. Both had their bows ready.

"So how did you get yourself arrested?" she was saying.

The bald man grinned. "Oh, that. Bit of an error of judgment." Dropping his voice so Galen wouldn't hear, he said, "I had a contract from the Watch. I was a licensed dealer. Any relics I heard of, I bought up, usually from farmers, and then sold on to the Watch. The profit was pitiable, but sometimes," he said with a wink, "sometimes I found something really juicy and held out for a good price. And of course, you can always get two castellans to bid against each other. They'll do anything to get a promotion."

Carys made a face. "You don't have to tell me."

He looked at her. "I'll bet you were some spy."

"The best."

"And you don't miss it?"

She winked at Raffi. "I'm still some spy."

Marco chortled. "Well anyway, I went too far. Found a pen that memorized what you wrote with it—amazing thing, still working. I sold it to one Watchhouse, but the sergeant at the other found out and had my business dealings watched. That was that. In days I was in the cells."

"That was where you met Solon?" Raffi said.

Marco glanced over at the older man. "Crazy old fool was giving away all his food to the others. If I hadn't looked after him, he'd be dead."

There was silence. Then Raffi said, "The Sekoi's taking a long time."

Carys shrugged. "That creature can scam its way out of anything."

He knew that. He'd felt the powerful hypnosis of Sekoi stories himself, the way they dragged you in, so you smelled and heard and lived the adventure. He wondered what yarns it was spinning in there. Kalimar and the Wyvern? The Last Stand of the Sekoi at Hortensmere? A clatter made him jerk suddenly. Galen leaped up. "Get ready."

The gate was being unbolted. They crouched, alert, Raffi suddenly afraid that the Sekoi's battered body would be thrown out onto the track.

The gate swung wide. A tall figure stood there with a lantern.

"Well, Galen?" it said irritably. "Are you coming?"

Relief soaked Raffi. And scrambling out, for a second he remembered Tasceron, the blind alley, the screaming, vicious attack of the draxi.

The Sekoi looked smug. Both gates were open; as soon as everyone was through, Galen and Marco dragged them shut, slamming home the bolts and the intricate sliding levers of the great locks.

"What about the men outside?" Solon muttered.

"Listen to you!" Marco scowled. "You're a soft-hearted wretch, even for a poor broken-down keeper."

Solon smiled. "I wouldn't want them to freeze."

"They weren't so concerned about us. They can knock,

Your Holiness, just like anyone else. Try not to shed too many tears."

Raffi looked scandalized.

Carys grinned. She could see the deep affection under the banter; it must have been all that kept the two of them sane in the horror of the Watch cells.

The Sekoi led them quickly over the bridge. The structure was wooden, and through the slits between the rough planks, Carys glimpsed the swift, dark rush of the water below. Their footsteps rang loud; coming to the north gatehouse the Sekoi turned. "Keep as quiet as you can."

Inside, the guardroom was spartan. Just like every other Watchpost, she thought acidly, recognizing the rotas and huge logbooks, the endless Rules painted in red letters down the walls, the meager fire with its tiny ration of wood. And that smell, so hard to name, so full of hateful memories.

The two men were near the fire. One was slumped on a stool, his arms folded on the table. He was staring deeply into the dull flames. The other stood, to Raffi's amazement, by the window looking out into the dark. Both seemed so normal, as if they were lost in thought and would turn around at once. But neither did. Their cross-bows lay on a huge weapons stack in the corner; Carys went over and helped herself to a pile of spare bolts.

"What story was it?" Galen asked, amused.

The Sekoi looked embarrassed. "These are crude men. It wasn't easy. Frankly, keeper, it isn't fit for your ears."

Marco sniggered.

"Let's go," Carys said.

"Wait." The Sekoi glanced swiftly at her. "I took the chance to search the place. On that wall are messages. Take a look."

Carys felt Galen crowd behind her.

The board held brief reports, probably brought by post-riders from the nearest Watchtower. Each one told of the same thing—Sekoi movements; small bands of the creatures, lone travelers, even whole tribes, all heading west on every road.

"What does it mean?" Galen turned.

The Sekoi bit its nails. "It must be a Circling."

"Which is?"

"A gathering. For something important."

"You knew nothing of it?"

"Galen, I've been on Sarres all winter."

Carys put her hand up to the board. In the top left-hand corner a larger notice had been torn off. The pin was still there, but only a fragment of white paper was left under it, with a few numbers that she stared at curiously. "I wonder where this went?"

"Why?" Galen looked at it.

"The numbers are the end of a code sequence. It was important—priority intelligence. Maybe direct from Maar."

"Don't you think we should go?" Raffi asked nervously.

"I agree." Solon was watching the men in fascination. "This is most strange. Will they remember seeing us?"

"They can't see or hear us." Galen dragged back the bolts in the opposite door. "They're deep in some sordid story. They'll only remember one Sekoi. Come on."

Once through both gates, they jammed the outer one with a fallen branch, hoping it would slow any pursuit. Then, without stopping, they ran. Galen led them straight off the road and up a steep track; they climbed high into the woods, hurrying in the dark along trails and paths that only keepers could sense, always up, out of the valley.

Breathless, Carys scrambled and climbed, wondering again at the Order's reckless way of travel, the way the group was strung out, Marco and Solon far behind. They had no discipline, she thought hotly, at least not the right kind. And yet Galen had his own defenses, and even she could almost feel his mind's deep entanglement with the wood, sensing far into its roots and soil and streams.

Finally, on the skyline among a high stand of sheshorn, they crouched and looked back.

The bridge was silent, the firelight a dim glow in the guardroom window.

"How long will it last?" Marco asked.

The Sekoi shrugged in elegant disdain. "With such feeble imaginations, maybe only an hour." It turned suddenly. "Galen, listen to me now. I think I must leave you. I need to go to this Circling and find out what troubles my people."

Galen looked hard into the creature's yellow eyes. Then he stood up. "If you must."

"I should." It hesitated a moment, then said, "In fact, I've thought since before we left Sarres that I should speak to my people. We have many sources of information. Someone may know something of the Coronet."

"You'll be discreet?" Solon said anxiously.

The Sekoi gave a mew of scorn. "We have no Watch among us, Archkeeper. But yes, I will."

"You can't go alone," Raffi said.

"Ah." The Sekoi looked awkward. It scratched its furred face. "I could. But then I would be out of touch with you. Even the . . . Even Galen could not reach me."

Galen nodded. "Then we split up. One of us comes with you. The rest go on to the observatory and wait for you there. Agreed?"

"Agreed."

"I think you should take—"

"I want Carys to come with me."

There was a moment of surprise. The scarred moon, Pyra, came out among the trees, glinting on the Sekoi's sly eyes.

"Great," Carys said. "Kind of you to think of me. Is this some sort of revenge?"

"Call it a challenge. A chance to learn something of the Sekoi."

She looked at it narrowly. Then she nodded. "All right. If you're sure."

The Sekoi smiled. "I am."

Galen said, "Get to the observatory as soon as you can. If plans change I'll . . . let Carys know."

Solon smoothed his silver hair. "I fail to see how."

"There are ways." Galen's eyes were dark. He gripped the Sekoi's shoulder. "Take care. Both of you."

The creature nodded. Then it turned to Raffi. "I'll take my belt now," it said with a grin.

Two miles on, they separated.

The Sekoi slipped into the trees and Carys followed. Before the darkness swallowed them she turned and made a face, waving at Raffi.

"Cheer up," she called.

Uneasy, he waved back.

14

Once, they say, Agramon came down and took a walk through the world, dressed in rags. She came to a town and asked for a room at a tavern. "This is all I have," she said, showing a purse with one coin. Beneath her coat the glimmer of her dress was silver. The greedy innkeeper winked at his wife.

"Is that so?" he muttered.

Agramon's Purse

THE WEATHER GOT STEADILY WORSE.

For three days it rained without stopping, a bitter sleet that made all the tracks quagmires; and on the fourth Raffi crawled out of exhausted sleep in a broken sheepfold to find the world white, every tiny blade of grass crusted with spines of frost. All that day, trudging over open fields, he felt the stricken shock of the soil, frozen in trampled ridges, all the tiny sprouting seeds seared and dead.

Everything was wrong. There was nothing left to eat. Solon was suffering from his Watch-injuries but walked steadily, uncomplaining. Each of them was soaked to the skin and could not get dry. The sense-lines had to struggle deep to find life; in every bare hedge and frozen stream all the energies had withdrawn, the creatures huddled and hidden, the embryos unborn. There was no spring—it had been shattered. And at night the skies were black, the stars frosty, the moons oddly brilliant in their colors and crescents.

Galen was worried. Late that evening, after the Litany, he looked across the meager fire to Solon, and Raffi knew what he would ask.

"Is this weather Kest's work?"

"I fear it, my son." Solon leaned back against the tree, rubbing anxiously at the dirt on his hands. "When Kest tampered with the Makers' creation, he began something that has never stopped. Only the efforts of the Order held the world in balance, but with our hold broken, the Unfinished Lands will soon overwhelm us. In twenty years or less. Perhaps this evil spring is the beginning."

"Didn't the console say something about the weather?" Raffi spoke quietly; Marco was a little way off, looking out over the fields beyond the copse.

Galen glanced up. "Yes. 'The weather-net holds' were

the words. And then 'We'll leave the Coronet active as a stabilizer.' "

He sat in shadow, but as he said the Maker-words, even casually, a rustle of power stirred around him, something so vivid and yet gone so quickly Raffi could only pray Solon had not noticed it.

If he had, the Archkeeper controlled his surprise. After a moment he pushed a branch farther into the flames and said, "Perhaps the weather-net isn't holding anymore."

"You mean the Makers could control the weather?" It was a new idea for Raffi.

"They made the world, boy," Galen growled in disgust. "All of it. If the Coronet is . . ."

Something snagged in Raffi's head. He hissed with the pain of it. "Sense-lines!"

Instantly, they were listening. Men. A whole group. Riding fast.

"Marco!" Solon warned.

Galen was stamping the fire out. The bald man rustled hurriedly back between the bushes. "What?"

"Watch! Get down!"

All at once the night was an enemy, prickling with

danger. Flat under the hazels, praying there were no vesps, Raffi felt the old terror surge up in him. He could hear them coming, galloping hard along the farm track, and under his forehead the thunder of hooves made the ground vibrate and shudder.

It took all his willpower to raise his head a fraction and look out.

A full patrol, maybe more. They were well-armed, the moonlight catching swords and bows, a few helmets swinging from saddles. In the dark it was hard to see much more, but they were riding at speed; even as he watched, they had crunched across the stream and were gone, racing in a long column up the farther fields.

Galen rolled over. He dragged leaves from his hair.

"Something's going on," he said. "The Sekoi know. The Watch know."

"And you don't?" Marco mocked.

Galen gave him a dark stare. "I know where we can find out."

⟨⋊⋉⟩

The Vortex

THE NEXT AFTERNOON they lay under the hedgerow and looked up.

The town of Arreto was built high on the hilltop. One road wound up to it that they could see; there were probably others. It had a strong-looking wall, with bastions. Inside that, Raffi could see roofs and parapets, and the Watchtower near the broken dome of what once must have been a shrine of the Order. From the dull sky the wind whipped sleet against his face. His breath smoked with the bitter cold.

"This is a terrible risk," Solon muttered.

That was no use, Raffi thought. Galen thrived on risks. He sometimes wondered what the keeper would have done in a safe Order, an Order that was rich and unthreatened, its disciplines rigid and unbroken. Set off for some remote edge of the Finished Lands, probably, or been martyred trying to convert the Sekoi.

"If you want," Galen said, turning his head, "you and Marco can go around. Raffi and I will go through the town and meet you beyond, where the road turns north to the observatory."

Solon looked rueful. "My son, don't tempt me."

"What about you, dealer?"

Marco laughed. "I know you'd like to get rid of me, Galen. But my stomach says no."

Raffi scowled. Why did he have to mention food? It was lack of food that had brought them to this; they had eaten all their supplies and there had been little in the frozen fields to forage. Marco had shot a wood pigeon, but that had been two nights ago and he had eaten it alone; neither Solon nor Galen would touch it. Raffi had even tried begging at a few farms, but the raw spring was obviously bringing famine; he had been seen off at all of them, and even now the thought of one great ox of a man roaring abuse in the doorway made him sweat.

This was populated country, full of Watch, crisscrossed with roads, busy with trade. Dangerous. And yet they had to pass it. Beyond the town the observatory lay on the slopes of Mount Burna, only two days' walk. But first they needed food. And information.

They waited till night to scale the walls. Galen had selected his spot carefully, where a crag jutted above a stream; it was fairly easy to climb up, though Solon

slipped once. Close up, the wall was rough and ram-
shackle; in places it had collapsed and slithered away, the
mortar dry and crumbling between the stones. Watch-
patrols passed across the top at regular intervals; when
one was out of sight Galen climbed up, crawled through
a gap, and vanished.

Seconds later his hooked face peered out of the shadows.

"Come on."

Raffi came last, bruising his knee and scraping his
wrist and finally dropping down onto a wide, dim ter-
race. Without a word they ran across it, the light of four
moons suddenly silvering them, and pattered down a
small stone staircase. They found themselves in a narrow
alley. On each side were tall, dark buildings, the sky a
strip far above where flittermice screeched. The alley was
silent, cobbled, leading downhill. Trying to walk casually,
they followed it.

Raffi felt lightheaded with tension and starvation.
After so long out in the wilds, towns were alien places,
crowded, full of secrets.

The alley led onto a street, past shops. One had food

sizzling outside; at another a potter was packing up, carrying in huge urns and vases.

Raffi smelled the cooking, painfully.

At the end of the street they came to a square. Trade was ending for the day but there were still plenty of people around, a few carts being loaded, someone selling cut-price flagons of wine. Marco bought one with his last coppers and they crouched under a colonnade and drank thirstily.

"What now?" Solon muttered.

"We could steal some food," Marco said. Catching Solon's eye, he grinned. "You people! All right. Somewhere to sleep."

"An inn?"

Galen frowned. "Too risky. Besides, we can't pay."

"Yes we can." Raffi pulled something out of his pocket guiltily. "We've got this."

He laid it on the step and they all stared at it.

A gold coin.

Galen picked it up in disbelief. "By Flain, boy, if you've . . ."

"I didn't steal it. It must have fallen out of the money belt. It was inside my shirt."

The Vortex

The keeper flung it down. "It's not ours."

"The Sekoi wouldn't mind," Raffi said sulkily, knowing very well that it would mind most bitterly.

"You're a sharp one!" Marco reached out for the money, but Solon was already turning it in his scarred fingers. The Archkeeper smiled.

"It has come to us," he said. "Certainly that was the Makers' doing. If we sleep out in some alley, Galen, we risk being moved on, or taken up as vagabonds. And one night in a bed would ease my weary bones, I have to say."

Galen looked at him darkly. "If you're willing to take the risk."

Solon flipped the coin. "I've taken worse, my son."

AFTER A CAREFUL SEARCH they chose an inn called The Myrtle Branch, in a dim back street far from the Watchtower. It looked clean, and through the smoke fug from its windows they saw the downstairs room was quiet, with only half a dozen customers. Serving them was a young woman, looking tired and harassed.

"I'll do the talking," Marco announced.

Galen looked at him. "You will not."

"Still thinking I'll sell you to the Watch?"

"I," Solon said firmly, "will talk to her, and the boy will come with me. You two sit by the door and try not to look so disreputable."

He went in quickly, before they could argue, Raffi tripping over the step in his haste.

Solon was wise, he thought. Galen would have scared her, and Marco she would have distrusted, but Solon was polite and kindly and travel-worn, and soon she was fussing over him as if he were her grandfather, fetching a hot drink and helping him off with his pack. He winked at Raffi and eased himself down by the fire with a sigh, stretching his legs out, clots of mud falling from his boots.

"We're visiting relatives. You're my grandson, and those two are your uncles. We're all the way from Marnza Bay. Know it?"

Raffi shook his head.

"Never mind. With luck no one else will either."

Galen and Marco came over and sat down. "All right?" Galen asked, looking around. No one seemed to be taking much notice of them.

The Vortex

"Safe as houses." Solon held out his hands to the flames, looking happy. "She's even cooking for us."

Halfway through the meal, two Watchmen stalked in. Raffi nearly choked with terror, but after one glance Solon poured him a cup of ale, calmly. "We are in the Makers' hands, Raffi. Let their will be done."

Gulping it down, Raffi thought that in his own way the Archkeeper was as reckless as Galen. He picked at his food, glancing in the mirror as the two men questioned the ale-wife. She pointed over toward them.

Raffi's heart thudded.

He couldn't swallow. The palms of his hands were slippery with sweat.

"If they arrest us, go quietly," Galen murmured. "Outside we can do something."

But the Watchmen nodded, took another look around, and went out. Raffi breathed out in silent relief, but Galen's eyes narrowed.

"We seem to be lucky," Marco whispered, lifting his cup.

The keeper looked at him. "Too lucky," he said.

They were given an attic room for the night.

A bed was wonderful, even if it was only stuffed with straw. Raffi threw himself on the nearest and rolled over, one arm over his eyes, as Solon went to close the hangings on the windows.

"Tomorrow," Galen said, dropping the relic bag down in one corner, "we spend the rest of the money on food and leave as soon as we've asked about Watch movements."

"I'm not sure, my son, that that will be possible."

Something dry in Solon's voice made Raffi sit up. He went over to the window and stood beside the old man, looking out.

What he saw made him groan.

The roofs of the town were already white.

It was snowing. Hard.

15

Like a bear to honey,
Moths to the flame,
We seek our destruction.
We have not learned how to be happy,
How to stop our headlong rush to death.

Poems of Anjar Kar

SOLON WAS WASHING.

He had stripped to the waist and Raffi could see the scars on his back and hands; horrible, twisted marks. He soaped himself in the hot water he had begged from the ale-wife, meticulously rubbing every inch of his skin. Maybe it was all that time in the cells, Raffi thought, that had made him so obsessive.

"He could go straight to them!" Galen raged.

"He won't." Solon groped for the towel. "He's an outlaw."

"Not if he sells us for his freedom."

"My son." The Archkeeper crossed the creaking

boards and caught Galen's arm. "You are sometimes like a tortured soul. Be still. I know Marco better than you do. He's a rogue and a heretic, but he and I suffered in the same chains. He won't betray me."

Galen folded his arms. "I pray to God you're right."

"Which is exactly what we should be doing." Solon pulled his shirt on over his head. Then he glanced back. "You have little fear of the Watch. But you have a deep hatred for what you think Marco is. Beware of it, Galen."

Silent, Galen nodded.

They said the morning Litany, Raffi making the responses in a sleepy voice, wary of listeners at the door. Overnight the snow had fallen heavily; now it lay deep over the little town, clogging the narrow streets.

As they finished, Marco wandered in, chewing a large piece of bread.

"Breakfast is ready."

Solon and Galen glanced at each other.

"So that's where you've been." Solon climbed to his feet.

"Where else? Chatting up the ale-wife. Her name is

Emmy. She's got three small sons and her husband is away." He winked at Raffi. "She's pretty too."

Solon sighed. "Stop teasing the boy and lead the way. Sometimes I think I should have left you to the rope."

"Not me, Your Eminence." He glanced at Galen. "Just think how dull your life would have been."

After breakfast they decided to work in pairs; Solon divided the money and they went out into the snow. All down the narrow streets shovels were scraping, voices rang sharp as bells in the frosty air. The wind raced, sending cloud shadows over the white plain below. Galen glanced up. "The wind's rising."

"The weather is certainly strange," Solon mused. "We'd best keep enough money for another night's lodging. We'll meet you back at the inn."

Watching Solon and Marco turn the corner Raffi said, "Will they be all right?"

Galen's look was hard. "Solon thinks so."

Trudging after the keeper between the heaps of cleared snow, Raffi tried a few sense-lines, but the world seemed icy and blurred, and all he felt was a cat in the house they were passing, rhythmically licking its tail, over and over.

He bumped into Galen.

"Stay alert," the keeper snapped. He peered around a corner. "Any trouble, just walk away."

The market was busy. People were desperate to buy food in case the weather worsened; there was an air of panic and fear. Supplies were scarce and things were expensive; Galen had to haggle over prices. A few times he got into conversation with the stall-owners, and all most of them could talk about was the weather.

"Huge floods out on the Morna river," one man said, almost eagerly. "I've heard five villages are flooded, and a lot have died. On the roads east whole families are traveling: carts, oxen, the lot. They've had tidal waves on the coast and in Imornos sixteen people were killed when freak lightning struck a Watchtower and it collapsed on them. It's like the end of the world."

A few people nodded. One woman made the Makers' sign with her hand furtively; seeing Raffi had noticed, she walked quickly away.

A small woman selling dried fruit said, "Talking of the Watch, I've heard they're after someone big. Hush-hush."

Galen frowned. "Keepers?"

The Vortex

"Who knows." She poured raisins into a small sack. "My brother supplies the Watchtower—he says they've had reports the Sekoi are migrating. They're no fools."

They could find out nothing more. By midday the wind was gusting, flapping the faded awnings and chinking flag-ropes in their metal rings. Galen drew Raffi into a doorway. "Before we go back, we'll check the shrine."

Raffi closed his eyes in despair. "Galen . . ."

"I know. But we have to make certain no relics are left there. It's our duty." He pushed past, swinging the bag over his shoulder. Raffi stared after him. He imagined Carys standing nearby and said to her, "He's mad." She grinned. "Go on, Raffi. You made the choice."

THIS SHRINE WAS AT THE END OF an alley that had been completely blocked with snow. A narrow trail had been dug for half of it, but then the snow lay thick and untrodden. Wading into it, Raffi felt the packed crystals crumple under his boots. In places it was waist-high, and he was soon soaked and bitterly cold, the strange gusty wind plucking at his coat. He clenched his fists, trying to keep the holes in his gloves together.

On each side deserted buildings rose, every ledge and architrave edged with snow. Light showers of it drifted down on him. Trudging along the street he saw all the doors were barred, the windows shuttered. In the houses nothing moved but spiders.

"This whole area is empty," he said uneasily.

"Good." Knee-deep in a drift, Galen dragged his coat tighter. "No one to bother us."

There were wide steps leading under the portico of the shrine; Galen crunched up them and tried the door. It was locked.

The wind moaned over the rooftops. Raffi looked back nervously up the lonely street.

"Around the back." Galen half turned, then stopped. There was a broken panel in the base of the door. He crouched and pulled more of it away. It left a hole.

Not a big hole.

Galen looked up.

"Don't tell me," Raffi muttered. He dropped on his hands and knees and peered in.

The Vortex

The darkness smelled of damp, a strange musty stench.

"Don't take long," Galen said.

Raffi laughed mirthlessly. Then he squeezed his head and shoulders through the gap, squirming in. There might well be traps, he knew. Drawing his knees up he crawled farther and straightened, trying to see in the dimness. From the cracked dome a pale snow-light drifted down.

"All right?"

"So far."

"Take a quick look. I doubt there'll be anything, but it's possible. I'll watch the street."

Carefully, Raffi groped in the dim interior. Rubble lay strewn on the marble floors; he tripped over smashed furniture and a great charred heap of wood where someone once had made a bonfire. Reaching into it he pulled out a broken statue of Theriss, her face half gone. Chilled, he thrust it back.

Something slithered over the floor.

He turned, listening.

Around the building the wind howled, confusing his sense-lines. All he could feel was decay and loss, a great bitterness of despair. A door was slamming far down in the corridors below, and bleak daylight pointed one long finger through the broken dome, lighting soiled frescoes of Soren and Flain high on the walls.

Their eyes had been hacked out.

Raffi clutched the fingers of his gloves. He was desperate to get out. But first he had to look.

Between snow-dusted rubble he clambered to the apse. Here was where the relics would have been, stored in gilded chests around the curved wall. But most of the chests were smashed, the floor below them shattered as if some great battering ram had been used. The last one was intact, but opening it he saw nothing but a mass of darkness inside.

A small black moth fluttered out and landed on his sleeve. Wind rattled the doors.

"Galen?" he whispered.

No answer.

He brushed the moth away but it drifted back, and two more with it. They were coming from inside the chest. Wondering if anything was at the bottom, he put his hands in.

The blackness rustled.

The Vortex

With a gasp he jerked back and saw it was made of moths, millions of them. In a great cloud they swirled out, fluttering onto him, clinging to him as he beat them away. They were on his face, his neck, and as he squirmed and dragged them off, he felt to his horror all their millions of wings swarming over his mind, clustering like a weight, a rustling darkness piling on top of him. He tried to yell, but the sound was muffled; he couldn't see, couldn't breathe. The moths smothered him; as he fell to his knees, the seething mass of furred abdomens and tiny antennae crawled into his clothes and sleeves, into his mouth and nose so he coughed and choked on crumpled bodies, their wings clogging his throat.

"*Galen!*" he screamed, sending the mind-call out, but the moths smothered that too; there were so many of them, their tiny malevolent minds hissing with the instinct to bite and suck. He beat feebly now, writhing, curling up on the floor knowing only the great mass clustering all over him; he was a blackness of moths, more and more of them till his mind darkened and his choked breath stopped, pulling him down a warm tunnel where he could sleep, deep in the weight of wings.

"Raffi!"

The yell was in his head.

Light broke over him, sense-lines like whips of pain that made his whole body convulse and jerk and cough. He was hauled up roughly, yanked upright, bitten and sore, retching.

All around him the air swirled. Moths filled it like dark snow, fluttering, in his eyes and hair, resettling even as Galen dragged him to the smashed door. His face and neck stung, he felt sick and giddy; but as he heaved himself out, the cold wind shocked his mind into clearness.

Galen stumbled after him, a drift of moths crisping from his clothes.

They ran down the steps and crumpled into the snow.

Raffi spat out fragments of wings, coughed them up, shuddering with cold and shock.

"Dear God!" the keeper raged. He staggered up, black hair blown in his eyes by the wind. He looked wild and furious; Raffi grabbed his coat.

"Don't."

"Don't what?"

"Whatever you're thinking of. Don't."

The Vortex

Power cracked down his arm, sharp blue sparks of it.

"I should burn it," Galen snarled. "As it ought to be burned! Not leave it like this, defiled, a nest of Kest-horrors."

"And bring every Watchman in the town down on us!"

Galen clenched his fists. "I could burn the whole town, Raffi! All of it!" He glanced down and it was the Crow that Raffi saw, a black restless shadow enveloping them both, charging the wind with energy.

"I know," Raffi breathed. "I know you could. But it would be wrong. We don't want vengeance, Galen."

Galen closed his eyes and wrapped the coat tightly around himself. "Sometimes," he said, his voice hoarse and bitter, "sometimes we do, Raffi. More than any-thing."

IT WAS DARK when they got back to the inn, the wind roaring now, gusting them against walls. Galen was limp-ing and they were both in pain from the bites of the moths, even though Raffi had tried rubbing melted snow on to cool the irritation. With nightfall the town was deserted, all doors and windows barred against the rising storm, but to their surprise the inn room was full.

Some sort of urgent discussion was going on. Many of the people looked like refugees, newly arrived. As Galen and Raffi pushed their way in, they found themselves at the back of a crowd, the heat of the room stifling after the chill air. A great fire burned in the hearth, and a stout man on a stool next to it was talking into an attentive silence. Raffi slammed the door, forcing back the wind. A cold draft roared the flames; a few people turned and looked at him.

Galen moved quickly to the staircase opposite, but Solon reached up from a small table by the window and caught his arm smoothly.

"Thank God," he whispered. "Where have you been?"

"Busy," Galen growled. "Where's Marco?"

"Gone to look for you. I think you should listen to this."

"I'm not . . ."

"Please, Galen. It's not good."

"The filthy Order," the man by the fire announced crisply, "have got to be responsible."

The Vortex

Galen turned instantly.

"You've no proof of that," a woman said bitterly.

"What other explanation is there! The weather's gone mad. You've all seen that. Now the Watch, have they got the power to do something like this? Do they have the knowledge?"

The crowd murmured. Someone waved for more ale; the woman, Emmy, brought out a fresh jug.

"Who is he?" Galen snarled.

"Some troublemaker. Keep calm. It's just Watch propaganda."

But Galen wasn't calm. Raffi knew that.

"I think we should go upstairs," he said, pulling Solon's sleeve urgently.

"Be quiet," Galen snapped. "I want to hear this."

"The Order are sorcerers." The stout man spat into the fire. "And believe me, there are still plenty of them, despite the talk. They have all manner of secret hideouts. And spies everywhere."

Raffi swallowed, his throat dry. The wind screamed against the shutters.

"They've put a spell on the weather. In revenge, there's

no doubt. They want to terrorize us all into fearing them. The Order always ruled by fear, we all know that . . ."

"*No!*" Suddenly Galen's pent-up anger exploded. He pushed Solon back and shoved through the crowd. "No! The Order ruled by love!"

"Love!" the stout man scoffed. "It was lies, all of it! Flain and the Makers! What did they make? The world? The world grew, friend, like a seed."

Solon was on his feet. "He's an agitator," he muttered. "The Watch use them to provoke rebels."

"We've got to get Galen away!" Raffi was desperate. "You don't know . . . You don't understand . . ."

"The Makers lived!" Galen roared, lashing a chair aside. "And only the Order kept the world from chaos!"

Power was almost visible around him, the flames of the fire leaping up. People backed off; one man opened the door and slipped out. The stout man looked alarmed. He got up from his stool and pulled a knife.

"Who are you?"

Outside, the wind shrieked. A shutter flew open with a crash that made Raffi jump in terror. The stout man stepped back, the stool smacking over.

The Vortex

"You're from the Order," he breathed.

Galen smiled his bitter smile.

"No!" Raffi shoved forward. "Listen!" he yelled. "Everyone! Listen to the wind! It's not just a gale. It's like a vortex!"

As if to answer him, a blast shattered the door wide. Straw swirled, the fire flattened and roared. All the windows burst inward in an explosion of glass and wood, and Raffi felt himself flung against Galen, grabbing the keeper's shoulder, feeling the sparks of energy as they crashed against the tables. Women screamed. Pots and dishes flew.

"It *is* a vortex," Galen whispered.

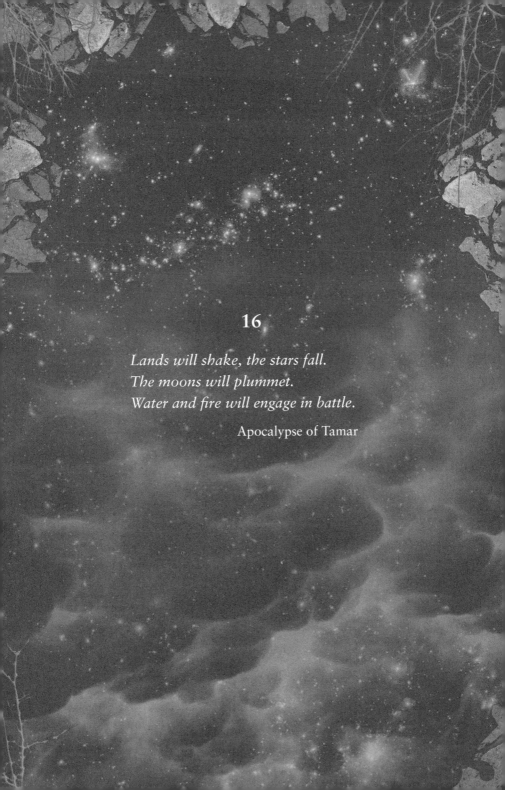

16

Lands will shake, the stars fall.
The moons will plummet.
Water and fire will engage in battle.

Apocalypse of Tamar

THE VORTEX MUST HAVE STRUCK the town full on. Deep in the dim cellar, huddled among casks and barrels, Raffi suffered its fury, the terrible wind shrieking like nothing he had ever imagined, the pain of it cutting through his mind like a knife, no matter how close he hugged his arms around his head.

They were well below ground, and yet even here the crashing of walls and buildings came to them as the storm smashed whole houses and streets. Dust showered down, but the roaring terror had long drowned all talk. Some children whimpered. A girl slept, exhausted. In the dull light of two snatched oil lamps,

Raffi glimpsed all their shadowy faces; dirty, tired people huddled in corners, who had managed to scramble down here when the inn roof had finally been torn clean away.

The stout man lay against one wall, holding a bloody rag to his head. They seemed to have been here forever. The noise was unbelievable; Raffi was sure nothing would be left standing. Closing his eyes he remembered briefly the smothering moths, the broken dome. That would have all gone. Galen's fierce urge to destroy it had been fulfilled.

Turning his head, Raffi glanced over at the keeper. For him the pain must be a worse agony, screaming along the raw sense-lines, but Galen sat still, his back against the damp bricks, his gaze steady and absorbed. As usual in times of crisis he could go deep into meditation, his soul far off. For a moment Raffi let himself wonder if Galen's rage had caused the vortex. Then he shook his head. That was stupid.

Solon sat next to him, his head pillowed on a sack. The Archkeeper looked gray and wan. He managed a smile. "Can't last much longer," he whispered.

The Vortex

An enormous crash shook the walls. A woman gasped. "Flain help us," someone breathed.

Suddenly bricks and stone came thumping down, a slither and thunder that made Raffi flatten himself in terror, and sent a vast cloud of choking black mortar through the cellar. For a moment he was sure the ceiling was coming in. A lamp toppled and smashed, spilling oil. Solon covered his filthy hair with his arm. "Tamar guard us," he kept muttering. "Soren protect us."

Slowly, the rubble slid to a stop.

The new, tilted darkness tasted of grit; Raffi spat it out, his whole body tense. This was terror; he breathed it in with the dust. It stifled his thoughts like the moths; that terror of the roof coming down, the crushing weight of the rubble above.

He curled tight, trying to think of anything else. Where was Marco? Dead, almost certainly. He imagined him, bleeding under some smashed wall. And Carys, and the Sekoi? Had the storm struck them?

He wouldn't think about that.

And then he realized he was listening to silence.

Utter silence.

Heads raised. Solon's prayers faded. Someone said, "It's stopped."

The silence was a great peace, a lifted weight. They could even hear the faintest plip of water dripping.

"Thank God," Solon whispered.

Raffi went to stand, but Galen's hand reached out and caught him like a vise. "It hasn't finished," he said, and his voice was harsh, filling the stifling space. "The center of the storm is passing over. We're only halfway through."

The ale-wife, Emmy, came crawling through the rubble. She was filthy, her long hair dragged out of its pins. She looked appalled. "Are you sure?"

"Certain." Galen looked at her. "Keep the children close to the walls."

They waited. The stout man mopped his wound. "If not the Order's work, keeper," he said stubbornly, "then whose? The Makers?"

Galen eyed him. "The decay of it."

"So what can save us?"

"Faith."

"In the Makers? They're long gone."

"Are they?" Galen glanced at him sidelong. "But you

The Vortex

were right about some things. The Order are not finished. The Order will save you, despite yourselves. So will the Crow."

As he said the word, the storm crashed back, an explosion of noise. Raffi groaned, covering his head. He lay there and endured it, knowing it was worse, louder, unbearable because a woman's crying was mixed up in it and from some dark despair he raised his head and saw Galen had an arm around Emmy and she was sobbing endlessly, her sons clinging to her. Time ended; only the storm's scream lived. Once Raffi thought the battering rage had lessened and he almost slept, in sheer exhaustion, and another time he wandered into delirium and knew, instantly and surely, that the Margrave was behind him, a grinning dark horror at his shoulder, as he screeched out and jerked around. But there was only Solon, looking old and somehow shriveled, rubbing at a tiny mark on his hands, over and over.

Raffi reached out and held his fingers gently.

The Archkeeper looked up abruptly. "The cells were like this," he breathed, his voice choked.

An icy chill touched Raffi's mind. For a moment he saw

a pit of horror; clutching the old man's fingers, he said, "This is not the cells. You're with us now."

Solon closed his eyes. When he opened them something had passed. He patted Raffi's arm and managed a smile, weary and kind.

And then, infinitely later, hours later, Raffi must really have slept, because when he opened his eyes and hissed with the ache of his stiff arms, the vortex had passed, and gray daylight filled all the chinks and cracks of the cellar.

PEOPLE WERE MOVING. Galen gently eased Emmy aside and scrambled up, dust streaming from his clothes and hair. Another man joined him.

"The stairs are blocked."

Galen nodded.

In the corner lay a great mass of rubble. The upstairs must have totally collapsed, Raffi thought in despair, but Galen had already clambered up and was tugging carefully at it. After a while he said, "I think we can get through, but it will take time."

He pried a stone out and handed it down.

The Vortex

They made a chain of workers, even the stout man joining in desperately as the glimmer of daylight above Galen's head widened, and Emmy tapped one of the casks into an old beaker, handing it around so everyone could drink. It was thirsty work, and dangerous. Twice stones fell in on them. By the time Galen could squeeze out of the gap Raffi's face was smudged black and his hands were sore and cut.

The keeper climbed up and disappeared. They heard the slither of rubble. When he looked back in his face was grim.

They lifted the children out first, then the others. When it was Raffi's turn to crawl up into the chill gray morning he shivered, staring around in disbelief. The town was gone. In its place lay a landscape of ruins, walls barely shoulder high, stairs that led nowhere.

People were picking over the desolation aimlessly. In places plumes of smoke rose up. Alleys and streets were lost under mounds of stone and plaster.

Solon stumbled out. He was deeply moved; there were smudges in the dirt under his eyes. "Dear God," he said. And then, "My poor Marco."

But there was no time to stare. Galen gathered everyone around.

"We clear the stairs," he said. "And use the cellar for the wounded. There'll be plenty. We also need water."

"The well." Emmy looked about hopelessly. "It was in the courtyard. Somewhere over there."

"Then we find it."

All morning they worked, at first with their bare hands. People from nowhere came to join them, some carrying injured friends, others desperately searching for wives or children. How many had died or were still trapped Raffi dared not think. Pausing once with a basket full of rubble he gasped to Solon, "The Watchtower will have gone."

"Assuredly. But anyone left will send for help."

By late evening the cellar was open. Fires had been lit and the well cleared, but food was scarce. Galen sent out foraging parties—it was strange how even the stout man, Andred, took his orders now without a quibble. Raffi went with them, finding what had once been a bakery and managing to scrape up some spilled flour and stale loaves.

Coming back into the warm gloom of the cellar he

squeezed past the rows of injured and saw a thickset man bending over the pile of packs in the corner.

"Marco?" he gasped, astonished.

The bald man turned instantly. He had the relic bag in one hand and the seeing-tube in the other. Raffi's grin of delight froze; he dumped the food and raced over.

"Raffi!" Marco said brightly.

Raffi snatched the bag. "What are you doing?"

Marco shrugged. After a moment he held out the relic-tube. "Perhaps I should say . . . "

"You were stealing them!"

"Raffi, look. I didn't know if any of you were alive."

"You could have asked!" Furious, Raffi crammed the relic back in the bag. "When Galen finds out . . ."

"Ah." Marco looked apprehensive. He glanced around at an old man being helped in by two girls. "Galen's busy. He's got a disaster on his hands. I don't think we need to bother him with my little mistake." He sucked a grazed knuckle, looking over it at Raffi. "Come on, lad. I won't go near the things again. No harm done."

Red-faced, Raffi glared at him. Before he could answer, Solon's voice, full of joy, rang over the rubble.

"Marco! My dear son! This is a miracle! An absolute miracle!" He scrambled down, slipped and grabbed Marco to steady himself; the bald man hugged him with equal delight. "I thought the wind had blown you away too, Holiness."

Over the Archkeeper's shoulder he winked at Raffi, who scowled and dumped the bag back in the corner. He knew he was defeated. If he told Galen, it would only make things worse. They had to keep Marco with them. He knew about Sarres.

Raffi turned, and saw Galen had come down the steps. The keeper was watching them. His gaze was bleak.

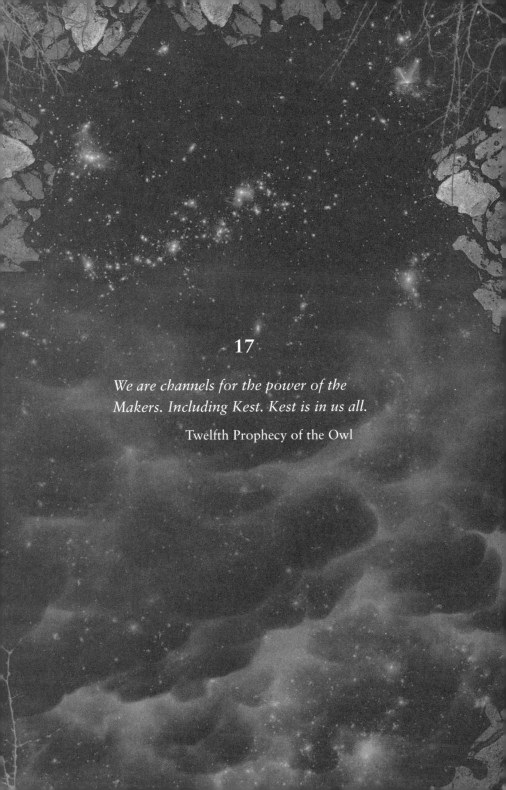

17

*We are channels for the power of the
Makers. Including Kest. Kest is in us all.*

Twelfth Prophecy of the Owl

Y NIGHTFALL THINGS HAD SETTLED, though Solon and Emmy and some of the others were still hard at work with the injured, bandaging wounds, setting broken bones. Moans of pain came from all corners; Raffi had to steel himself not to shut them out. There were few medicines, and many people had been dug out with severe injuries. More were still trapped.

The night was cold but clear. All seven moons rose in it, and as he snatched a rest from helping with the digging he gazed wearily up at them, longing for sleep. He tried vaguely to open his third eye and make light patterns, but all his energy was gone, drowned out with the strain of

243

the endless terror of the wind. And then with a sudden vivid shock he saw it, and stared, amazed.

"Get on, Raffi!" Galen yelled. "There may be people still under here!"

"I know. It's just . . ." He looked from Cyrax to Atterix, then back to Agramon. "The moons are wrong," he breathed.

Silent, close behind, he felt Galen's astonishment. They said nothing. There was nothing to say.

Of all the knowledge of the Order, the patterns of the moons were what any scholar studied first. The patterns were eternal, year in, year out, the sisters' long complex dance through their chain of movements—the Web, the Arch and, most holy of all, the Ring, formed only once a decade on the feast of the Makers' Descending.

But now they were wrong. Agramon was wrong. She should have been overhead, a thin crescent, but she was too low and, it struck Raffi suddenly, too big.

"Agramon is falling!" he whispered.

Galen pulled him out of sight behind a battered roof. "Say nothing! Try not to keep looking up." But he stared up again himself, his sharp profile against the frosty sky. "Dear God, Raffi, this is worse than any of us had thought! Agramon is out of alignment. The skies themselves are slipping into chaos."

"*Galen*!" It was Marco's yell, urgent. With a glare of warning Galen grabbed his pick and scrambled over; Raffi followed hastily.

"Someone's alive down here." Marco was lying in a hollow of rubble. "Listen!"

A whisper of sound was muffled under the stones.

"We'll get you out!" Marco called. He glanced up. "How many?"

Galen came down beside him. "Two. But we need to hurry."

It took an hour to reach her. Each time they called, her voice was weaker. Emmy talked to her nonstop, pushing her arm deep among the stones till she could feel the cold fingers grasping hers. A heavy beam from a collapsed ceiling had held off most of the crashing bricks but the woman kept gasping for them to hurry, because of the baby. Always because of the baby.

"He's cold," the choked whisper came up. "So cold!"

Galen looked anxiously at Solon. "I can barely sense it now," he muttered.

In the freezing night everything went chill. Then Marco began to dig faster, recklessly. "Get more torches," he yelled, flinging a stone up to Raffi. "And blankets."

The cold clouded their breath. Ice was forming on the rubble, beautiful and deadly. In the flaring light of the torches Marco's eyes were red and sore in his filthy face. "I can see her!" he hissed.

As the rubble came away, so could Raffi. A woman lying under the beams, in a tangle of smashed wood.

"Take him!" she gasped, pushing something white up into Marco's arms. "Please!"

Marco turned to Raffi. "Get him to the fire," he said, his voice oddly strained.

Because the baby was dying. As soon as the tiny head fell against his chest Raffi knew it, and looked up, stricken. "Galen!"

Flame light flickered around him. "Lay him here," one of the women whispered.

It was a boy. They wrapped him hurriedly in warmed

The Vortex

cloth but he was blue in the face and barely breathing, his tiny eyes closed and filthy with dust.

Emmy bathed his face carefully. "What can we do?" she muttered.

Marco and Galen were dragging the woman out. The stones slithered dangerously but she tore herself out of their grip screaming, "Darry! Is he alive?"

The baby gave a faint croak as Emmy bent over him, massaging his chest with her fingers. "He's going," she whispered.

"*No!*" The woman grabbed the child. "He can't die!" she screamed, her face a mask of agony. "For Flain's sake, help him! Can't anybody do anything?"

No one answered.

And then Solon pushed forward. He came up close to her, his hair silver in the moonlight, and he held out his hands.

"Give me the child."

His voice was so calm that after a second she obeyed. Solon took the tiny form and laid him down in the nest of blankets. "Get them all to move back," he said, glancing up at Marco. "Right back."

As the bald man pushed the crowd away the mother crouched. "What are you going to do?"

Solon looked at her kindly. "Nothing, daughter. Whatever is done here, the Makers do it."

She closed her eyes with sudden weakness.

"I may need you, Galen," Solon murmured.

He closed his eyes.

For a long second there was only stillness and the crackle of the flames. And cold. A cold that struck deep into them, the icy chill of death, unmistakable, hardening over their hearts as it frosted the ruined town.

Until Solon spoke.

"Flain," he said, his voice raw. "Tamar, Soren, Theriss of the Sea. Kest of the Sorrows. Hear me. Put the breath back in your child. Put the light back in his soul."

The baby had stopped breathing. Even Raffi knew that.

The crowd shifted, restless. "What's he doing?" someone called.

Solon touched the child; forehead, chest, and palms, breathed on him and handed him back to his mother.

"Praise be to God and the Makers," he said quietly.

And the baby screamed. His voice rang out, a fretful

The Vortex

hungry wail loud over the frosty ruins, scattering rats and skeats, sending flittermice screeching off like shadows.

The crowd surged forward. The woman, sobbing with joy and astonishment stared at the child, clutched him tight, kissing his head over and over, but Solon just turned and walked toward the cellar.

People fell back, making a way for him. The night was full of some terrified delight that Raffi could almost taste. Galen strode after him and Raffi followed, his sense-lines suddenly charged with energy as if it had risen through the earth.

In the cellar, Solon sat unsteadily by the fire.

Galen crouched before him. "Are you all right?"

"A little tired, my son. Nothing more."

"I'm not surprised!" Galen shook his head. "Tallis was right. You have a rare gift."

Solon shrugged and smiled up at Raffi, who said, "It was a miracle!"

"No, lad. The Makers put their strength back into him. I was only the channel."

"The faith was yours," Galen said. "But tell me, when you invoked the Makers, why include Kest? For healing?"

Solon stared at him. For a moment he seemed almost shocked, his breath clouding in the frosty air, and something like a vacancy passed over his face. He looked lost and bewildered. "Did I?" he whispered.

Then he grabbed Galen's hand. "Listen, I have to warn you . . ."

The words choked, dried up.

Worried, Galen held his arms. "What is it?"

All the sense-lines rippled. For a second something black and terrible stood among the three of them, a flicker of evil that came and went like the leap of a flame. Solon looked around hopelessly.

"It's gone. I thought . . . But I might have been wrong. I'm so tired, Galen, that's all."

"We all are." Weary, Galen sat down by him, stirring the fire up. It was very dark in the cellar now; most of the injured slept.

Abruptly Galen said, "I have something to tell you myself. Solon, you asked me once how I broke the ice at the Frost Fair." He dragged both hands through his long hair. "It's difficult to explain. The boy and I were in Tasceron."

Solon was watching, with suppressed excitement. Raffi

knew he had been waiting for this a long time. "You can trust me, my son," he said gently.

"We found the House of Trees. It still exists, Archkeeper, deep below the ruined streets. And in the House we found . . . the Crow."

Solon looked astonished. "Alive?"

Galen was silent a moment. Then he said, "The Crow is a relic. A device to speak through. For a few seconds we spoke with the Makers, Solon. So far away, they sounded. And so close. And then . . ." He shook his head, Solon caught his arm.

"Tell me, Galen," he said fervently. "I feel a terrible struggle inside you. Tell me what it is."

Galen looked up, sudden and bleak.

"I am the Crow now, Solon. The power of the relic burned into me. It lives deep in me like a spirit; sometimes it surges out like a wave of energy." He smiled grimly. "That was how . . ."

Then he stopped.

A brick had slid from the rubble; someone stood there. The flames crackled in the wind and leaped up. Solon sighed bitterly.

"Marco."

The bald man came out of the shadows and crouched to get warm. He stared at them both curiously. "I didn't mean to listen. I don't suppose you believe that."

Galen stared back in cold fury. "You heard?"

"Everything." Marco shook his head. "I never thought I'd have this sort of luck and not be able to use it. What would the Watch pay for the Crow!"

Galen's eyes went cold, but Solon smiled. "Don't tease us, old friend."

"Oh, I won't." The bald man spread his hands and grinned at him. "Both of you are too much for a plain man like me. You'll have to trust me, Galen."

But Emmy had come clambering in, with Andred behind her. Her face was white. "Hurry!" she gasped. "You must go, all of you!"

"The Watch are here," the stout man muttered. "A column of forty riding hard toward the town. You can see them from the walls."

Wearily, Solon stood up. "But there's still so much to do here."

"For us, not you," the man said, his voice harsh. He

glanced at Galen. "I'll think differently about the Order after this."

As they turned away Emmy caught Galen's sleeve. "Listen," she whispered. "They know about you—the Watch. They knew you were keepers, but they warned me not to alarm you."

Galen stared at her. "How! How did they know?"

She shook her head. "I can't tell you."

In five minutes they had grabbed the packs and a handful of food, and were at the walls, where the vortex had smashed an enormous breach.

Raffi looked back at the ruined town. "What will they do?" he murmured to Galen.

"The Watch will clear the place. Make its people refugees and beggars," the keeper said harshly, watching Solon press the last coins into Emmy's hand. "It's no good to them after this."

"But there are people still buried . . ."

Galen turned on him in wrath. "Yes, there are! And don't you know the Watch by now, boy! They'll leave them to die." He rubbed his face with the back of one hand in exhaustion. "As we're leaving them, God forgive us."

Cage of Stories

18

"My people were deceived by the Makers and enslaved by the Watch. You can imagine we have been wary since then. If we keep secrets we have our reasons. If they think of us as animals, without minds, so much the better."

Words of a Sekoi Karamax.
Recorded by Kallebran.

CARYS LOOKED AT THE MAP in bewilderment. It meant nothing, and turning it up the other way didn't seem to help. The Watch had always taught that the Sekoi had no writing, but there were certainly letters on this; unreadable, spiky signs all down one side. She threw it aside in disgust and glared at the plate of dewberries. That was another thing. She was sick of dried fruit.

Scrambling up, she walked out of the cave.

Before her the beach was smooth, the wet, ridged sand shining in the glimmer of the moons. Strange wooden posts stuck out of it in a long line, their wood bleached and split into bizarre spiny sculptures by the tides, and far off a faint wash of small waves rippled, a hypnotic sound.

As she was watching the Sekoi came up and threw itself down near the cave mouth, brushing sand irritably from its fur. Without looking up it said, "It's as we feared. The tribe tell me the weather is far worse to the north. There have been terrible snowstorms and floods, and three great vortexes. Millions of hidebeasts have begun to move down from the hills, trampling the fields."

She sat down. "I hope Galen and Raffi are all right. Did you find out anything else?"

"Little."

She glared at it. "Don't lie to me! You've been gone hours!"

The creature sighed, narrowing its yellow eyes. "Carys, my people speak through their stories. I have been reliving their journey. Unlike you Starmen, we do not rob our words of all their echoes and senses."

Carys smiled sourly. She sat and leaned back against the rocks, dipping her hand into a tiny moonlit pool.

Cage of Stories

Suddenly phosphorescent shrimps scattered in panic. "What about the Coronet?"

The Sekoi shifted, awkward. "I have asked. No one knows for sure. But I have discovered why the Circling has been summoned."

"The weather?"

"In a way." It pointed with the longest of its seven fingers into the sky. "And for that."

She craned her neck back. "Agramon?"

"Agramon. Do you notice anything strange about her?"

For a moment Carys was still. The complex phases of the moons was not a subject the Watch thought important for its spies, but she knew the familiar patterns well enough. "Shouldn't it be a bit higher?" she said at last.

The Sekoi nodded. "Indeed. The moon you call Agramon is out of position. My people tell me it has been slowly drifting among the stars these four nights, each night a little farther. Or a little nearer."

Appalled, she turned. "You mean it's *falling*?"

"Who knows? This much is clear—that Galen's vision

on Sarres was a true one. From the observatory—if it still stands—it may be possible to see more clearly."

"Then we should get back!" Carys tucked her dyed hair behind one ear. "We need to tell them!"

"I suspect they know by now." The Sekoi made no attempt to move. Instead it stretched its legs out and said quietly, "I'm surprised you didn't."

Carys stared. "What's that supposed to mean?"

"I think you know."

"Well, I don't. Stop hinting. Say what you've got to say. You could start with why you were so keen that I came with you."

The Sekoi looked over to the campfires on the beach. "Very well," it said, its voice dry. "I brought you with me to get you away from Galen."

She sat up slowly. "What?"

"You heard. Cast your mind back to the river. That terrible beast that nearly devoured poor Marco. How lucky that was, Carys! Because without it we would never have dared the bridge, and I would never have found the truth out about you."

It turned then and looked at her, its eyes sly in the

moonlight, and instantly she felt a prickle of danger that amazed her, all her instincts wary.

"Me? What about me?"

"That you have betrayed us."

She hissed her breath out in irritation. "Are you still wittering on about that! I've told you, I'm finished with them . . ."

But the Sekoi was not listening. It had reached into an inner pocket of its coat and now pulled out a white piece of paper with one corner torn off, which it unfolded with long fingers.

Carys stopped. "What's that?"

"You may well look perturbed." The Sekoi's fur had thickened around its neck, a sure sign of anger. It looked at her steadily. "This is what I took from the notice-board of the Watchhouse."

Carys clenched a fist of sand. "You took it!"

"I did." Its eyes were slits of yellow malice. "Listen to this, Carys Arrin. Though I don't think it will astonish you as much as it did me."

Holding the sheet so that the moonlight fell on it, the Sekoi read the words in a dry, hard voice:

PRIORITY INTELLIGENCE.

TO ALL WATCHTOWERS, GUARDPOSTS, ROADBLOCKS, AND SUR-VEILLANCE UNITS. TRAVELING NORTH, ON FOOT. A GROUP OF SIX, DETAILED AS FOLLOWS: HARN, GALEN: KEEPER . . .

Carys gasped. The Sekoi ignored her.

MOREL, RAFFAEL: KEEPER. KARNER, SOLON: KEEPER. FELANIS, MARCO: THIEF AND RELIC-DEALER. ARRIN, CARYS: WATCHSPY. SEKOI, NAME UNKNOWN. DESCRIPTIONS FOLLOW.

It glanced at her over the paper.

"But how could they . . . ?"

"There's more.

ROUTE: ASKER FIELDS, WYREN VALLEY, POSSIBLY ARRETO. DES-TINATION: MAKER OBSERVATORY, MOUNT BURNA.

NOTE: IT IS VITAL THIS GROUP BE ALLOWED TO PASS WITHOUT HINDRANCE. NO, REPEAT NO, ARRESTS OR INTERROGATIONS ARE TO BE MADE. NO SURVEILLANCE NECESSARY. INSIDE INTELLIGENCE AVAILABLE.

"What!" Carys shook her head. "That's impossible."

"Indeed. Yet someone has told them our names and where we're going." Maddeningly calm, the creature folded the paper. "At the bottom," it said acidly, "is simply the word *Maar*."

Cage of Stories

Instantly, Carys leaped. She flung two handfuls of sand full in the Sekoi's face, rolled, jumped up, and ran—straight into the aimed sights of a crossbow.

Her crossbow.

"Keep very still," growled the tawny Sekoi who held it.

She froze.

All around, in the cave-shadows, in crevices, up on the cliff top, the tribe had gathered. They watched her in silence, their strange eyes unblinking. Behind her the Sekoi spat out sand and wiped its eyes.

"Nice try," it snarled wrathfully. "Come back and sit down, Carys. We're a peace-loving race, but we despise the Watch, and if I gave the word you'd be shot without mercy. That would be a shame—after all we've been through together."

Ignoring its sarcasm she turned and stalked back, feeling the hostile gaze of the tribe. She felt utterly confused; she *had* to think straight. She sat down. "So there's a traitor in the group. But it's not me."

"Despite this little escape bid?"

"That was a mistake." She tried to stay calm and continued, "I know when I'm being trapped. But listen.

Did you show that notice to Galen?"

"I did not." The creature scratched its tribemark calmly.

"Why not?" Carys exploded.

"Because he would not believe it of you. He trusts you. I've remarked before that he is vulnerable because of this faith of his. He believes he has changed you, and you're happy to let him think that. And yet all the time . . ."

"All the time nothing!" Furious, she leaped up, ignoring the taut bow at her back. "You stupid fool! Don't you realize what you've done? You're so anxious to blame me you just haven't thought! I'm not the spy. So it has to be someone else. Someone still with them!"

"You mean Marco or Solon." The Sekoi nodded. "I have considered that. But you see, Carys, Galen distrusts Marco and will never let him know anything important. For instance, neither Marco nor Solon know about the Crow . . ."

"Yes, but . . ."

". . . And there is one sentence on that paper I haven't read to you. The one that convinces me the traitor is you." She stood stock-still. In the moonlight the Sekoi's glance was sharp and melancholy.

"What sentence?"

"Simply this. After Galen's name it adds: THIS MAN IS ALSO KNOWN AS THE CROW."

In the utter silence the lap of the sea seemed nearer. Far out over the dim waves, a mew-bird squawked.

Carys sat down as if her legs had given way. She was so astonished she could hardly speak. "They know about the Crow?"

"I think you'll agree," the Sekoi said tartly, "that lets off Marco. And Solon. There's no one else. Unless you think Raffi is a spy?"

She scowled at it. Then her face lightened. "Alberic! What about Alberic and his gang! They know!"

Just for a second the Sekoi frowned. "That one. But how would he find out where we are now, or that our destination is the observatory? Only we six know that. And if the Watch know it, they know everything. About the Crow. About the Coronet. And about Sarres." It looked at her and its voice was a hiss of sudden bitter anger. "How could you do this, Carys? After all the Order has suffered? And Sarres! If I ever get back there and find Felnia gone and that sweet island blackened by Kest's taint I will never forgive you for it. Never. Because it has to be you."

In despair she glanced around. The tawny Sekoi with the crossbow had crouched. Now it stood up again.

"What are you going to do?" she said coldly. "Kill me?"

The Sekoi looked disgusted. "I'm going to find Galen. You will be kept here. In a cage."

"A cage!" She laughed bitterly. "Do you really think you people have a prison that can hold me? I was trained by the best."

"Indeed?" the Sekoi purred, icily polite. It drew its long knees up and leaned on them. "But we have, Carys," it said quietly, the ripple of the sea in its voice. "We have chains the Watch never imagined and a prison no one can break out of. Because the chains are stories and the prison is your own mind."

"*No!*" She leaped up instantly. "I won't let you do that to me!"

"There are too many of us," its voice said smoothly.

Cage of Stories

"And besides, we've already begun."

"*No!*" she screamed, grabbing at it.

But the Sekoi had faded into a rock and all the beach was empty.

The hand she held out was furred. And in her seven fingers she held a small basket full of clams.

19

"I suppose," the Wolf said, "I should be scared?" It licked its great teeth with a long tongue.

"You should." Pyra put down the clam basket and shrugged off the red cloak.

"Because I'm not what you think. And if you swallow me, all you'll get is a fire in your belly that will never go out."

The Wolf crouched. "If you don't mind," it said politely, "I'll take my chances."

"Fine. Whenever you're ready."

Pyra and the Wolf

ᴀND THE WOLF LEAPED.

"No!" Carys screamed in fury. "This is just a story!"
But the great maw opened and she was inside it, swallowed deep down red tunnels into a raw, pounding heat.

THE SUN WAS GOING DOWN. All the horizon was on fire and Herax knew the danger beacons had been lit; warning flames across the Karmor hills. Below her the Sekoi army was gathered, thousands strong, armed only with wooden staves, small knives, hastily cut spears. The

Karamax went among the columns, encouraging them, firming their minds with legends.

Beyond the fires, over the edge of the world, the Watchmen were. They moved in dark rows on the high downs.

Herax tuned the final string on the saar. She struck a soft chord, and the music went down into the veins of Anara, and shivered in the leaves of the trees. All the Sekoi-host heard it; it entered their stories and memories, seeping into them, a great unsettling, stirring their wrath.

Herax sang the Song of Anger; a wordless song, a song without harmony, that had not been sung since before the Starmen came. It moved through the host like anxiety, like an ache, darkening their minds; and as she sang it she felt her own thought curl up and her mind go cold with the chilling anger of the Sekoi, knowing it was her skill that would bring so many to their deaths. Herax . . .

But her name wasn't Herax.

She stopped, struck by that. Her fingers gripped the taut strings and she stared out at the smoky fires, not seeing them. Her name was . . .

Was . . .

It had gone. Shaking her head she flung the saar down

Cage of Stories

among the rocks. "No!" she snapped. "Not this story either. You'll never get me to forget! My name is . . ."

But there was only emptiness. And as the army in the plain below gave a great cry, rain pattered hard from the iron-gray clouds.

Bewildered, she watched it drip from her seven fingers.

THERE WERE TOO MANY STORIES. They came so fast; she slid helpless from one to another like a shadow, caught up in the fights, the journeys, the escapes. Breathless and injured in the Karelian jungle; then lazing on a bed of silk in the Castle of Halen; another time wandering deep in the Forbidden mines, consumed with nothing but thirst—all the scenes crowded in on her. And she lived them. They were real. She could smell the mossflowers that tried to devour her, taste the bitter chocolate in Bara's box. When the kite-bird struck at her in the tombs of Ista it made her bleed and hiss with pain, the thin amber stain clotting the fur of her neck.

Only now and then when a story drew to its close did the despair come flooding back, the sudden knowledge of the cage, so that she knew she was trapped in an endless web of words and events and happenings—old treacheries, love affairs, wars, quests—none of it hers, none of it mattering. And beyond that was something else, some deep real anxiety that bit her like a Kest-claw which she couldn't shake off, and in all the confusion of the stories she could never find out what it was.

Once, deep in the strange Sekoi-houses in the tale of Emeran from before the Watch-wars, she caught a glimpse of her own narrow striped face in the mirror and knew her name was Carys and that her eyes were brown, not yellow, but the knowledge was gone in an instant as the keeper Ganelian knocked on the door and the whole relentless tragedy began. She was Emeran; all that had happened to her had to be lived through, and only when the tale ended and she found herself weeping over his body with the poison vial in her hand did she struggle back to herself.

Just for a second, her mind cleared. She smeared the tears away fiercely, knowing she had to do something, now! But what? There was no Watch-training for this. No procedures. Old Jellie had never taught her anything about escaping her own mind. Galen would have. The Order, they understood things like this. They knew . . .

But it was already too late.

The story flowed back. She drank the poison, feeling its hot stain corrode her stomach and veins. As she fell forward, retching, the white Emeranflowers sprang out of the ground around her.

THIS WAS THE SEKOI-CONSCIOUSNESS. She saw with their eyes, smelled their sharp scents, dreamed in their odd, complex colors. The stories grew older, more alien. Now they were myths of heroes from before the Wakening, when the world was colder.

Standing on the rock of Zenath, tied hand and foot with the broken sword at her feet, she stopped struggling with the ropes and stared up at the sky, the wind flapping her long coat.

Because it was dark. Too dark.

Quite still, she wondered why the stars astonished her, what was wrong with them; ignoring the churning wash of waves as the great two-headed god strode toward her through the sea.

Then she realized.

THERE WERE NO MOONS!

The shock of it almost made the story fade. There were no moons, and the Anaran sky was black as she had never seen it, full of millions of brilliant stars.

And it was so cold.

This was important, she knew it was; she tried to hold on to it but the story surged back and the giant cried out, "Where is my sacrifice? Where is my reward?" so that the rock shook. She tore a hand free of the ropes and grabbed the sword.

"It's not me!" she screamed. "And I'm not going to fight you!"

But the god roared and swung its great mace and she ducked, striking back at it. For a day and a night she fought with it, time that passed without time, until Anarax rode to her rescue on the winged night-cat, and in an instant the story transformed and . . .

Cage of Stories

. . . SHE WAS STANDING ON A HILLTOP, still under a dark sky, with six other Sekoi.

Breathless, she looked up.

Out of the night, a silver staircase was forming. Down it came new, strange people; small, slender forms, their hair long, unfurred. A male first, tall and dark-haired, dressed in a coat of stars, and behind him others—a female, another bigger male with an animal in his arms.

The Sekoi murmured. Around her, anxiety rippled.

The Karamax walked out to meet the Starmen.

Under her feet the grass was frozen. As she crunched on it something shot through her numbed mind like a stab of memory. She had seen this meeting before. A hundred times. On smashed windows, images, relics. These were the Starmen.

Men.

She struggled for the other word bitterly, forcing her mind after it as it slipped away.

Makers.

These were the Makers.

The Sekoi gathered at the foot of the stairs.

"We welcome you, strange people," Sharrik said in the Tongue.

The Starmen smiled. The tall one held out small hands.

"Let us be friends," he urged. "My tribe and your tribe."

She knew this story, but it was wrong. This wasn't how Raffi told it.

Raffi!

How do I get out? she asked him, almost in tears. How do I direct the dream, Raffi, and get out of this stinking mess! What do I do?

But he wasn't there, and the Starmen were turning away. The story was fading and she knew she had to do something now, right now, or this would go on forever, so she shoved through the gap and ran, breathless, to the foot of the silver stairs and grabbed the cold handrail, screaming out the only name she could think of in an explosion of breath and anger.

"*Flain*! Wait! Talk to me!"

He stopped.

Halfway up the stairs he turned, as if he was puzzled.

She felt free, as if she had burst a hole in some smothering web.

Cage of Stories

"Listen to me, Flain, please! Galen always says I should talk to you. So now I'm talking."

He smiled. "I see." Quietly he walked back down. She saw he was a man in his prime; dark hair slightly touched with gray, hiding the thin gold crown. Close up, his face showed a small scar on the bridge of his nose, and the dark coat he wore was threadbare, flecked with small moth-holes.

She caught hold of his arm. "Tell me my name."

"You know your name," he said patiently. "It's Carys."

"Carys! That's right!" She frowned, scratching her furred tribemark. "Look, I need help. I have to break out of these stories!"

Flain laughed. "You've needed help before. You've rarely asked for it."

"That was different!" Looking up, she saw Tamar and Soren and Theriss waiting for him. Right at the back was a smaller man, thin and wiry, his narrow face bearded, closed with some inner tension. A chill of astonishment touched her. That must be Kest.

"Different?" Flain asked lightly.

"It was never like this!" She shook her head. "There

was never a time I hadn't been trained for, when I didn't know what to do. But this! It's all in my mind. I can't stop it. It won't let me out and Galen's in trouble, all of them are!" She had five fingers now. She threw down the Sekoi wand in disgust.

"And we, the Makers? We're in your head too?"

"That doesn't mean you can't help me."

He smiled wanly. "Remember that outside the cage, Carys, if you can. And tell the keeper he will see me soon. Very soon."

Suddenly she caught a glimpse of gold in his hair and put her hand up. "That's the Coronet!"

He stepped back.

"That's what we're looking for!"

He nodded. "Indeed. Gold." A long look passed between them; she caught her breath in sudden understanding. But he had turned and was walking up the stairs.

"Wait! How do I get out?"

"That's easy! Even Raffi could tell you. You just open your eyes."

"They are open!" she yelled, furious.

"Ah, but they're not."

Cage of Stories

A door slid wide in the sky. One by one the Makers went through it. On the threshold Flain looked down at her and smiled. "It's easy, Carys."

Then he stepped in, and the sky slid back.

At once the story began to gather; she could feel its power, speeding, crowding, moving her on, the fur on her face rippling back. She yelled with anger, shrugging off everything, swearing, struggling, kicking it away. "Wait!" she screamed at the stars. "What use are you? Come back and help me!"

No one answered.

So she gave up in utter exhaustion.

And opened her eyes.

20

Alas, who speaks in the silence now?
Who lights up the dark?

The Lament for Tasceron

AT FIRST SHE THOUGHT it was another story.

She was lying on her back, and all she could see was blue. After a moment she realized it was the sky. A mewbird soared across, opening its mouth as if it squawked, though Carys heard no sound. In fact, all she could hear was a faint hum.

She sat up, and stared around.

She was on a wooden slab in an empty room, and she was cold, but the amazing strangeness of the room made her forget that.

It was a bubble. An enormous clear dome of glass, coming right down to the floor all around, and as she stared out of it in wonder she saw that it rose up in the middle of the ocean, and all she could see out there on every side was water, a vast swell that slapped and surged against the glass, leaving swathes of foam that slithered silently down.

It was astonishing. She swung her feet off the table and stood up, finding her body stiff and aching. She was ravenously hungry.

But the dome! Walking up close she saw her own reflection, and putting a hand up she touched the glass. It was smooth and perfectly transparent, though it had to be incredibly thick. Not a whisper of sound came through it. Maker-work, obviously.

There was a small step up to a gallery that ran around it; and she climbed up, so that her eye-level was above the water. She was standing in the sea; it was all around her and yet she couldn't smell it or taste its salt. Miles of empty water stretched to the horizon, and the small moon, Lar, was just setting, a chalky smudge.

It looked to be about midday. But which day? And where was the land?

She shook her head. So much for boasting to the Sekoi.

Cage of Stories

Her pack lay under the slab and she hurried down to it, rummaging inside. She pulled out another shirt and dragged it on, hurrying her coat back over it, then unwrapped a few strips of salted meat and dried fruit and gobbled them down. There was a jug of cold water and a cup. She drank thirstily. Obviously she wasn't meant to starve.

There was no way to tell how long she'd been here. Days maybe. The Sekoi might even have reached Galen by now. Chewing raisins, she looked around the room carefully and saw the door, outlined in the smooth wall under the gallery.

She poured the rest of the water into her own flask, then swung the pack on fiercely. As she did the straps up, her hands shook with a fury that almost made her laugh. So she was a traitor, was she? She grabbed the crossbow, checked it, and loaded a bolt grimly.

At the door she glanced back. Spray slid down the perfect arc of the dome. For a second she imagined how it might be to stand here at night, in a storm maybe, the great swell crashing high, flinging spray over the tiny room lit only by Maker-lamps. Who had looked out from here all those years ago?

Not the Sekoi, that was sure.

"Thanks, Flain," she said. Turning to the door she touched the discreet handle. The door slid aside, soundlessly, just as the doors in the House of Trees had done. Cautiously, Carys stepped out.

She was in a corridor. It ran into darkness in both directions. A low, barely heard hum filled it.

There were no windows. Light came from tiny studs in the floor; as she walked over them they lit up, and those behind her went off again. Amused, she stood still. The lights stayed with her, lighting again as she walked, a ripple underfoot of pale glimmers. She had no idea if this was the right way. But it sloped down, and after a while the chill deepened and the walls became rock.

She was under the seabed.

At the end were some stairs. They were wide and the balustrade had been carved into ornate festoons of fish and shells. As she crept silently down, small lamps lit for her passing, held in the rigid tentacles of stone octopuses, slithering around the handrail.

At the bottom was a hall. It was enormous, smelled

salty, and the floor was covered with water. At first she thought this was some Maker-trick, but when she touched it with her foot it rippled; a shallow flood, right across the tiles. Under it eels seemed to slither, long watersnakes with raised fins, their colors blurring from green to turquoise in the gloomy light.

Carys splashed across. Was it supposed to be wet, or was there a leak in the roof? She quashed that thought and looked at the doors. There were at least eight. Choosing one at random she slipped through and stared.

She was in a gallery, and the whole roof and sides were made of the thick glass so she could see out, up through green depths of water. Terrified it might crack, and the vast implosion of ocean sweep her away, she stared up, shadowed by the creatures out there, great billowing rays, shoals of vivid fish, darting and flickering. Huge crabs scraped their shells soundlessly over the glass, and in places spiny coral had colonized it forming fantastic sacks and bizarre brittle structures that ribbon-snakes slithered through.

She wandered the gloom of the gallery in fascination, barely noticing the door at the end until it slid open with a hiss that made her whip up the crossbow, stepping into the darkness warily.

No lights came on. It felt like an enclosed space. She stepped forward and into something. A barrier. Gripping the cold tubing, she peered over, and bit her lip in awe.

A great pit opened in the floor. It plunged endlessly down, dizzyingly deep, as if for miles below. At intervals a ring of small purple lights glowed, so close to each other down there, they seemed continuous.

Giddy, Carys jerked back. She scratched her hair with cold fingers and laughed shakily. "The Sekoi certainly have secrets."

Perhaps her voice activated something. Because the lights instantly changed color. Far down in the depths a dim whine started up.

Carys ran. She panicked, racing back through a door that slid open into another corridor, then down it, her heart thudding.

When she stopped herself she gripped both fists and tried to think. The Sekoi had gone. So there must be a way out. It would just be a matter of finding it.

Half an hour later, she knew the place was a maze. It

must run for miles under the sea, surfacing here and there in strange atolls and domes. Weary and dispirited, she wandered rooms with vast lakes where mer-fish swam, and past a whole series of waterfalls that cascaded down walls. An entire chamber was built of mother-of-pearl, another of white bone like a whale's great belly. She stared up at it. It was as if she had been swallowed. And Galen was in trouble.

"Flain!" she yelled in sudden fury. "Were you only part of a story after all? How do I get *out of here!*"

She hadn't expected an answer. But as she swung away, to her horror, the air spoke.

"I thought you'd never ask," it said.

Carys whipped around. She jerked the bow up, taut.

"Come out," she snarled. "Slowly!"

"I'm afraid that's not possible." The voice sounded amused. "I can't come out. I'm not physically focused in quite the way you mean."

It was a cool voice, oddly difficult to identify. Not a man's. Or a woman's.

Carys backed to the wall. The room was empty. She could see that.

"Who are you?" she breathed.

"I am the palace."

"The palace?"

"Of Theriss. The Drowned Palace, the Sekoi call it, though that is something of a romantic fallacy. They're a childlike race. But better company than none."

Carys lowered the bow. "How can you be the whole palace?"

"In theory," the voice mused, "you are, of course, right. It is a misconception. However, that is how I'm referred to. Specifically I am the intelligence of the palace. Its systems. Is this clear?"

"No." Carys rubbed her hair and found it soaked. "Are you alive?"

"You do ask some interesting questions." For a moment the voice sounded sardonic. "That one could take some time to answer. Let's say I'm not a person as you'd define one."

"Not . . . one of the Makers?"

Then it did laugh, an echoing sound. "I love it when you call them that. Tamar would have roared."

Behind Carys a door swished open. She jumped and whipped the bow around but the voice said silkily,

Cage of Stories

"Shall we chat as we go? You did ask for the way out."

For a moment Carys hesitated. Then she propped the bow under one arm and marched out, head high, feeling very small and grubby.

"This is ridiculous," she hissed. "They couldn't have made the air talk!"

"They didn't, of course. This way. And hurry. I have to keep the power down."

The corridor lit up, a glimmer of pale light. Carys stalked down it in silence.

After a while the voice said acidly, "I appear to have annoyed you."

"It's just," Carys snarled, "that I've been wandering around here for hours . . ."

"Yes, I was aware of you. I thought . . ."

"You can see me?" Carys stopped dead.

The palace laughed. "You *are* a philosopher. I can't tell you what a change this makes. The Sekoi, bless them, tell everything in narrative. It takes so long! Their minds are not good at the abstract in any sense, though Flain told me once they'd be the real survivors. He'd be amused that they . . ."

"They brought me here." Carys walked on quickly. She felt totally at a loss; this was another situation the Watch had never foreseen. But she had to get as much information from this patronizing creature as she could.

"They did. I'm always happy to let them in. Though they have strange ideas."

"How long ago?"

"I'm sorry?"

"Since they brought me."

"One day, six hours, twenty-seven minutes."

"Flainsteeth," Carys hissed. But it wasn't as bad as she'd thought.

The palace laughed. "Left here. Watch the whirlpool."

Dark water gurgled down a channel deep in the floor. Carys sidled past it. "Did the Makers live here?"

"Not as such. It was their pleasure palace. Mostly they were based in Tasceron, though Kest . . . Well, never mind Kest. How is the dear old city?"

"Black," Carys said grimly. "Haunted. Soaked in eternal darkness. No one goes there."

There was silence. When the palace spoke again its

voice was oddly subdued. "The Sekoi told me that. I had hoped it was one of their tales."

"Well, it's not. Where now?"

"This way." Hurriedly, lights rippled on. Doors slid back. Carys saw a series of rooms opening in front of her.

"Your Maker-power," she asked, curious. "Is it running out?"

Above her something sparked. One of the lights snapped off. "*No,*" the voice said tightly.

"But you don't want to waste it, do you?" Carys looked up. "If it did all go, would you die?"

The voice laughed, mirthless. "There you go again." For a moment she thought it sounded terrified. "I really couldn't say. And Flain told me they'd be back; he insisted they'd be back, so that's all right, isn't it? Don't you think?"

"They told us that too," Carys said, wanting to comfort it.

"They did?" The relief was clear. "Well, there you are then."

She walked through the rooms. "Listen. Do you know anything about a relic called Flain's Coronet?"

"A relic." The voice sounded annoyed. "Now there's a

term I detest. Redolent of death, something left over. Left behind. I suppose you consider me to be a relic too?"

"I suppose so." Carys grinned, wondering what Galen would say. "But what about the Coronet?

"Flain wore it. Only when he needed to. It's a highly sophisticated neural integrator."

"A what?" Carys demanded.

The voice sounded superior. "Obviously it's a waste of time my explaining. It was used for a number of operations. May I ask why you want to know?"

"We're looking for it."

"Ah. Because of Agramon."

Carys stopped again. She looked around at the wave-painted walls. "You know about that?"

"I have certain viewpoints to the outside. Agramon is out of alignment. The Coronet is the only solution, if it still exists. Someone will need to put it on and enter the awen-field, but I don't think it should be you. You don't strike me as having the necessary—"

"Save it," Carys snapped. "It won't be me."

A door slid open.

To her astonishment she saw the beach, the smooth

sand with the waves beating on it. It was late afternoon, and raining torrents.

"This what you wanted?" the voice asked, smug.

"Yes," Carys turned hastily, trying to think what else to ask. "The Sekoi. How much do you know about them?"

"Not a great deal. They keep their little secrets. Though one of them once drank too much and blurted out all about the Great Hoard." The voice was scathing. "All that gold! It will do them no good at all. Do they really believe that Flain would . . ." It stopped.

"What?" Carys asked eagerly.

There was silence. Then the voice said testily, "It's so crazy I'd love to tell you. But I can't. Promised them I'd never mention it. As if there's ever anyone to mention it to! Well, good luck then."

"Yes," Carys said hurriedly, "but wait . . ."

"Pity about Tasceron," the palace muttered. "Perhaps I'd better run a full systems check."

"Wait! I want to ask you . . ."

"Another time. Have to keep the power down."

And the door in the rock snicked shut.

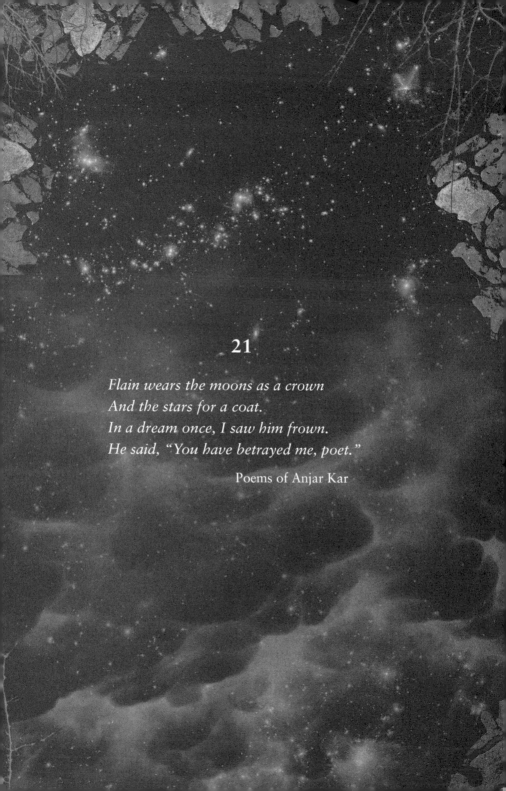

21

Flain wears the moons as a crown
And the stars for a coat.
In a dream once, I saw him frown.
He said, "You have betrayed me, poet."

Poems of Anjar Kar

RAFFI ROLLED OVER AND YAWNED.

The fire had burned low. Galen was leaning against the observatory wall, wrapped in his dark coat, gazing up at the sky. For a while Raffi lay still watching him. The keeper looked worn, as they all did. He rarely slept enough, and the horror of the Vortex had scarred him; Raffi felt it deeply in this moment of quiet, the terrible anger, the shame of having to leave those who needed him. All the power of the Crow seemed to have rolled up small and gone away; in the shadows of the evening Galen seemed as withdrawn as when the relic explosion had devastated him, over a year ago now.

"Something's wrong," the keeper muttered. He didn't look over.

Raffi sat up, alarmed. "What?"

"I don't know." Galen didn't move. "They know about us. And I can feel, sometimes, something wrong. Among us. A shadow among us. Then it's gone." He glanced over. "Have you felt this?"

Raffi nodded, thinking uneasily of Marco.

"I thought so." Galen looked back at the sky.

"Perhaps it's the weather . . ."

"They know about us." Galen stared through the gloomy plantation of firs. "Say nothing to the others. Here she is, at last."

Behind the dark branches Agramon was rising. The moon was always the largest, a smooth featureless disc tonight, but it should have been visible an hour ago. Galen climbed stiffly to his feet.

"Let's go up. Wake Solon."

They had slept all afternoon, but it wasn't enough. Solon groaned and rolled over, rubbing his stubbly chin. His pale eyes looked wan but he managed a smile. "Already?"

Cage of Stories

Raffi nodded and moved to Marco, but Galen said, "No. We don't need him."

He had opened the great wooden door. From inside, the smell of damp oozed out.

They climbed the stairs without a light, readying their eyes for the dark. As the tight turns made his legs ache Raffi wondered what material the Makers used that could keep this place intact after so long. The vortex had missed it, but earlier another storm had raged here. They would be lucky if the sky stayed clear.

The tower was empty. Sense-lines told him that. Animals had been here, but no people, not for years. There was a faint stir of something that might have been a Sekoi-trace, but though he groped after it with all his skill Raffi couldn't catch it and gave up.

At the top Galen stopped, one hand on the wall, head down, silent with the pain of his leg. Far behind, Solon toiled up patiently.

The room they wanted was the first one. Pushing the door open, Galen limped in.

It was made of glass.

A glass cube in the sky, and the windows looked so

thick, Raffi thought, reaching up to touch one. Instantly he jumped back.

"Carys! I saw her!"

She had been reflected, where his own shape should have been. "Reaching up, just like that!"

Solon had come through the door and was staring around. Galen frowned. "She may be thinking of us."

"This is intriguing!" the Archkeeper said, turning. "But Galen, there are no relics here! In fact, there's nothing here at all."

His disappointment chilled them, and he was right. The room seemed stripped bare. In the cold moonlight it looked abandoned. Agramon shone through the glass, throwing its light on Galen's face. He turned to look at it.

"We weren't sent here for nothing," he growled. He put both hands on the window.

Instantly, to their shock, it transformed. Something in the glass seemed to ripple; the image of Agramon shot closer, as if it plunged toward them.

Raffi gave a yell of terror; Galen snatched his hands back.

An enormous moon hung before them.

Then Galen laughed sourly. "I see."

Cage of Stories

"Has it fallen?"

"No, it hasn't, boy, and if you can't say anything sensible don't bother. It just looks closer. Like our tube, this glass has that property."

Solon winked at Raffi. "That's a relief. I wonder if I look as white as you."

Galen touched the glass again. He was concentrating, and Raffi knew he had linked his mind with the relic and was learning its ways, the image of the moon slowly receding to a pinprick, and then looming again, growing until it filled the window and he and Solon stood transfixed in fear and wonder.

It seemed so close!

Now Galen narrowed down the focus, and they seemed to be barely above the surface, traveling over it, seeing the stark smoothness of the globe, without hills or valleys or features, dry and dazzling with reflected light.

"It's not real!" Solon breathed.

"What?"

"Don't you see," the Archkeeper said in excitement. "The moon is not a natural thing! The Makers created it from their material; it is artificial, Raffi!"

Amazed, they stared at it. Then Galen nodded. "The Sekoi have tales that say there were no moons before the Makers came. I've always scorned them, but maybe they were right. Maybe the Makers formed all the moons and put them in the sky for a reason."

The thought of such power chilled Raffi to the core. When Solon spoke again his voice too seemed smaller. "Incredible."

"To us. Not to Flain."

Solon came forward. He stood beside Galen and gazed up, the ghostly light silvering his hair and coat. "I feel strange things," he said quietly. "As if there was a great field of power all around the world, finely adjusted, delicate as hoar-frost."

"The weather-net." Galen's hooked profile was dark against the moon. "And the movement of Agramon has disrupted it."

"Or the other way around."

"Look." Raffi pointed between them.

On the moon's surface broken domes were coming into view, made of the same pale stuff as the land, bubbling out of it like boils. Beside one a vast antenna stood.

Cage of Stories

The moon's drift slowed. Galen held the image, and closed in.

"The Coronet," he hissed.

"My son?" Solon glanced at him.

"There! Look at that!"

It was a pattern, marked out in great globes on the surface, some strange enormous sculpture. Seven globes, some small, some larger. Red and gold and pearl. Familiar.

"Where have I seen that before?" Solon murmured.

"It's the Ring! The circle of the moons. At least we've always called it that, but maybe it had another name once, an older name." Galen's voice was tense with joy; Raffi felt it surge in him. Instantly the screen blacked, and then as the keeper spread his hands wide over it, it crackled into bewildering life; rows of figures rippled over it, hundreds of numbers that shot upward in columns. Diagrams flickered, patterns and formulae gone in seconds, as if Galen had broken into some deep file of knowledge and was racing recklessly through it.

"What are you doing?"

"The Coronet!" Galen's voice was choked; he jerked

his hands back, but still the screen convulsed with symbols until one appeared that stayed and they all recognized it.

The seven moons in the formation of the Ring.

Galen turned, the power of the Crow rustling in his shadow. "That's it. Kar says it in a poem somewhere. The moons *are* Flain's Coronet."

He caught the Archkeeper's arm. "Think of it! The moons control the weather, the tides, everything on Anara. It's deep in them that the Makers' power is concentrated! There may be a relic that links with them—that's what we need to find—but the real Coronet is there in the sky. All the time, Solon, it's been in front of our eyes!"

Raffi swallowed, his mouth dry. Something snagged behind his eye. He blinked, but Solon was reaching for the screen in fascination.

"You must be right. And think what else this machine might tell us, Galen. How far can we see with it? Out beyond the stars, maybe, even to the home of the Makers themselves!"

Galen turned, impatient. "There's no time for that! We need to find the crown Flain wore!"

Cage of Stories

Solon stared at him. The older man's face was lit with a strange hardness of longing; for a second he almost looked angry. Then he rubbed his scarred hands over his face. "You're right. Forgive me. We must not allow ourselves to be distracted. I confess I . . ." He stopped. "There's someone here." He glanced at Raffi. "Isn't there?"

But Galen was already through the door. They ran after him, sensing the man in the other room, the door crashing open. Racing in, Raffi glimpsed Marco's swift turn, his yell of fear as the keeper grabbed him, broken pieces of Maker-work falling from his hands.

"Galen!"

The keeper slammed him against the wall, eyes black with rage. "I should kill you now," he snarled.

Marco slew his head sideways. "But you won't," he gasped, trying to grin.

"Since the beginning you've been an evil weight on us!"

"Don't blame me that you had to leave those people," Marco spat. "Blame the Watch. Or shouldn't the Crow be able to make it all better with one magic word?"

Galen hissed. He hauled the man up and struck him hard in the face.

Marco staggered, pulled back and whipped a long knife from his belt.

"*No!*" Solon cried. "Stop this!"

"Stay out of it, Holiness. It's been coming a long time."

"Galen! I insist!"

The keeper was silent, breathing hard. There was a terrible wrath in him; it churned like a black pain. Even though he knew Galen's temper, Raffi was appalled at the depths of this; it was an abyss, like the dark between stars, like the pits of Maar.

Marco crouched, his hand waving the knife. "You may have your own weapons, keeper, but that's never stopped me. I'm waiting."

In the charged room no one moved.

Then a cool voice spoke from the doorway. "I'm afraid you'll have to wait. Galen, it's not him you have to worry about."

Raffi whirled around.

The Sekoi stood there, looking travel-worn.

Galen didn't move. "Isn't it?" he said, his voice hard.

"No, it isn't. And we don't have time to waste." It walked right up to them, took the knife swiftly from Marco's hand, and tossed it down.

Confused, Raffi looked at the door. "Where's Carys?"

"Not here, small keeper. I've got things to tell you that you won't like, Galen, but first we have to leave this place. At once. The Watch know we're here."

Galen turned and looked at it. He seemed barely to understand, his eyes still black with anger. "How?" he asked.

"Later. We need to go. I've sent messages on—they'll be waiting for us."

"Who will?" Solon asked.

The Sekoi scratched its fur, yellow eyes sly.

"My people. At the Circling."

CARYS MOVED QUICKLY. A few miles inland she found a village and stole a horse, riding it relentlessly north all night. In the rain it was hard to tell direction; she used her old Watch lodestone and grinned as she thought of Jeltok's boring lessons.

For hours she pushed on, through mud and rutted tracks, climbing into the hills. The horse was a poor beast; by early the next morning it was too winded to do more than stagger, so she sold it heartlessly at a roadside farm for food and directions, then set off on foot, half running, in the Watch pursuit pace.

The Sekoi had a day's start, but it must have gone on foot. She had to catch up with it. Fury drove her, fury at herself and it. Of course the creature didn't trust her. Why should it? Why should any of them, after all the tricks she'd pulled? And who had told the Watch about Sarres? Because the Sekoi was right. That could finish them.

Scrambling wearily through wind-blasted woods and flooded fields she brooded on that, their one safe place lost. It drove her on through exhaustion and mud and swarms of bloodflies and the aching stitch in her side. She had to find Raffi. She had to tell him it wasn't her.

At midday she limped past a cave, low on Mount Burna. A man came out of it and stared at her. She gripped the crossbow tight.

He looked like a hermit, gray and starved, his hair clotted and uncut. A wildness about his eyes warned her. A string of small bones rattled around his neck.

"Has a Sekoi passed this way?" she gasped. "Gray, striped?"

The man clutched his ragged sleeves. He seemed witless, so she strode on toward the trees, but after a second his voice drifted after her, hoarse and strained.

"There are none left, not anymore."

She turned, wary. "What?"

"There are none anymore."

For a moment she looked at him. His skin was crusted with dirt. The bones chinked. From the cave a pregnant skeat wandered out, yelping.

"None of what? Tell me what you mean."

He shook his head, his eyes filling. To her horror he clawed at his face with one hand, leaving long scratches of blood. "They're gone," he whispered. "All of them. All lost, all dead. There are none anymore."

Carys stood rigid.

Then she turned and raced into the trees.

All afternoon she climbed, not looking back, desperate to get the madness and despair out of her mind.

By sundown she knew she had to be close, but the fog had come down, yellow and rancid-smelling. It closed around her, blurring the gloomy plantation of firs to complete darkness, so that all she could do was keep climbing, breathless and sore and ready to scream with frustration.

Until she saw the light.

Nebulous and vague, it hung above the treetops, fog wisping over it in drifts.

It had to be the observatory.

She struggled through sharp branches, tripped over humps and anthills, then slammed suddenly against something hard.

A wall.

Groping around, she found a great door ajar, and slid inside. Fog filled the damp stairwell; she raced up, hearing the murmuring of voices, an argument, a thump high above.

The door to the top room was open; breathless she walked straight in.

Talk stopped.

All the men sprawled about the room turned to stare at

Cage of Stories

her. Each of them wore the black uniform of the Watch, and they smelled of beer and sweat.

Carys turned like lightning.

The man behind the door had already kicked it shut.

He grinned, showing black gaps between rotting teeth.

"Well!" he leered. "And who's this then?"

The Circling

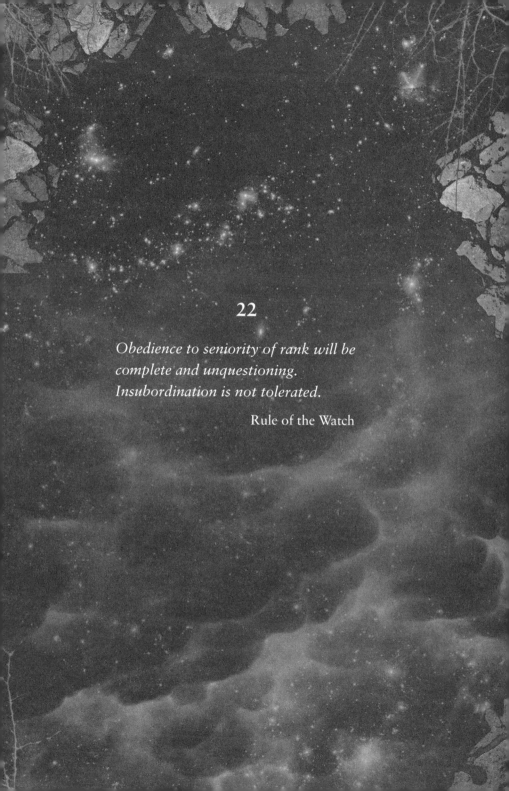

22

*Obedience to seniority of rank will be
complete and unquestioning.
Insubordination is not tolerated.*

Rule of the Watch

NO ONE SAID ANYTHING.

Strange oily rain cascaded in sheets from the clifftop beyond the overhang. The Sekoi folded its long fingers and waited.

It was Raffi who exploded. "She wouldn't! She'd never have gone back to them!"

"She's never left," the Sekoi said calmly. "The wanted list is an age-old ruse." It flicked an anxious glance at Galen. "I'm sorry. I know you thought . . ."

"She rescued Galen from the Watch! And Sarres! She loves Sarres! She'd never betray it." Raffi leaped up. He couldn't bear this. "And she's not even here to argue for herself. How could you leave her in some dream? She'll die!"

"She won't." The creature grimaced. "And I left her because I will not risk taking her to the Circling."

Raffi gave a hiss of disgust. He walked to the edge of the overhang and stared angrily out into the crashing rain.

Still Galen had not spoken. He looked bleak.

Solon said hesitantly, "Of course I did not know her as well as you. She always seemed . . . astute."

"As sharp as a needle," Marco muttered. "I always suspected there was no way out of the Watch." He folded his arms. "Still. At least now you know it wasn't me."

Galen ignored him.

"It is Sarres I mourn most." Solon rubbed his hands together thoughtfully. "The Watch riding in there . . ."

"They won't." Galen's voice was harsh, but Raffi was relieved to hear it. Thunder rumbled over the wood below, a long crumpling roar, startlingly loud.

"But . . ."

"They won't. Sarres is not a place but a state of belief. No one can find it without faith."

"I did," Marco observed, sucking a tattooed knuckle.

The Circling

Galen didn't bother to answer. He got up and went over to Raffi and stood behind him, looking out into the storm.

"It's not true," Raffi whispered. "We'd have known."

"Not if the Margrave controlled her," Galen said bleakly. "She may not even have known herself."

Raffi turned, horrified. "Some sort of mind-link?"

"It must be. We didn't know. And the Margrave has the power of Kest in him. Who knows what sort of abilities he has. She left no messages, talked to no one. How else could she have done it, Raffi?"

"It wasn't her." Stubborn, Raffi turned back to the rain.

He wouldn't let himself think that it was.

CARYS STARED DOWN AT the grinning face. She knew at once that if she showed the slightest fear she was finished.

"Get on your feet when you address me," she snarled.

The Watchman didn't move. His grin flickered, then widened. "The girlie's got a temper! Why should I?"

"Because soon I'll have you hanging by your thumbs in Maar for blowing the biggest undercover operation since Tasceron!" She whirled around. "Who's in charge?"

A gray-haired man took a bite from a marsh-pear. "I am. And—"

"Shut up and listen. I need a horse and I need it now." She tugged the insignia off her neck and tossed it to him; he had to scramble up to catch it. "Carys Arrin. Five forty-seven Marn Mountain. Priority Bulletin twenty-six/page nine hundred, dated two weeks ago. Remember it?"

Something changed in his face. "I might."

She walked right up to him, furious. "You should. You're the patrol that's been following us. Right?"

He nodded slowly. "But you're on the list. You're supposed to be—"

"Flainsteeth, do I have to spell it out?" she hissed. "I'm in Harn's group posing as a renegade agent. How else do you think the information's getting out!"

He glanced over her shoulder. She heard the others getting hurriedly up and felt suddenly exhilarated. She was enjoying this, she realized. At last it was something she knew how to handle.

She snatched the insignia back from his hand. "I need to get back to them before they get to the Coronet." Pushing past him, she helped herself from the Watch rations on the table, shoving food into her pockets.

"Where are they headed?" he asked, too casually.

Carys laughed, scornful. "And you think I'm telling you! My orders are to report straight to Maar. No one else."

"Told you that would be it," one of the others muttered.

She turned on him. "What?"

"How Maar knew so fast. We couldn't work it out. Thought it might be the fur-face, doing some kind of mind-talk. Those beasts have all sorts of tricks." He looked at her curiously. "How do you do it?"

"That's my secret. What are your orders?"

"Follow Harn's group, but stay well back," the sergeant said. "And neutralize this place." He looked at her, and his scrutiny was hard and uncertain. "So why aren't you still with them?"

"The Sekoi suspected me. I had to deal with it." She prayed they hadn't come across the creature, but the Watchsergeant just nodded.

"At Arreto there were only the keepers. But won't they . . ."

"Not if I catch up to them." She turned abruptly and marched straight to the door. "I want the best horse. And get this scum out of the way."

The black-toothed man spread his hands. "No hard feelings," he said with a grin.

Carys looked at him narrowly. "What's your number?" she said, cold.

His face went white. "Six oh four. Sor Lake."

She nodded. "I'll remember that."

At the bottom of the stairs the fog was thicker, but when they brought the horse she climbed on and turned it quickly. "They were well gone when you got here?"

The Watchsergeant nodded. "Tracks go west. Into Sekoi country."

She nodded. Without a word she urged the horse on and galloped into the fog.

Five minutes later, hands shaking, she had to stop. For

The Circling

a moment weariness washed over her, a shuddering relief
that drained her of all energy, so that she crouched low
and breathed deep, dragging the sour smog into the back
of her throat.

Then she pushed the hair off her face and listened.

Behind her, glass was being smashed.

Pane after pane of it.

RAFFI HAD NEVER BEEN SO DEEP into Sekoi country. He trudged wearily after Galen, watching the keeper's
stick stab the sodden red soil. The weather deteriorated
now with astonishing speed; crashing rain drifting into
an acid, stinging snow, then into squalls of howling wind
with bizarre airborne showers of small, brown toad-like
creatures that he had never seen before. A while ago a
flash flood had roared down the valley, sweeping broken trees and even boulders along in its torrent. Now the
night was dry and icy and there was a faint tang of fog in
his throat.

There were no birds, few animals. Everything was hiding. He had never sensed a land so cowed.

They walked, silent; Galen was too morose or too deep in prayer to speak and whenever Marco ventured some comment he ignored it.

"And everything I say just makes things worse," Solon had muttered mournfully during a pause to drink. He flexed his scarred fingers, pouring water over the dirt on them and rubbing it anxiously. "I am deeply sorry about Carys, Raffi. It must be hard for you. You were good friends."

Raffi looked sick. "It wasn't her."

The Archkeeper was quiet, replacing the cork. Then he said, "When I was chained in the Watch cells, those under torture dared not speak to one another. You never knew who was a real prisoner and who was a spy. It was one of the worst things. You dared not say anything, comfort anyone, ask a question. And outside too it can be like that. Even if they're not listening, we think they are. That's what they've done to us."

Behind them, Marco laughed. "You talked to me."

"And you to me, old friend." Solon turned, passing the water flask. "In the end we have to trust each other. That's the only thing that will outwit them." He put his

The Circling

hand up to the awen-beads that were gone, his fingers searching for them absently. "Dear God, what dark times those were. What horrors we endured . . ."

Marco lowered the flask. "Don't," he said sharply. "Stop thinking of it." He caught Solon's wrist and pulled it down. "It's over. All over."

For a moment they looked at each other. Raffi glimpsed a shared despair, a sudden pitful of shame and terror that he jerked back from, embarrassed and hot.

"It'll never happen again," Marco said firmly.

"My son." Solon put both his hands on the other man's shoulders. "We both know very well that it might. If they capture us, we will pay for our escape."

Now, watching Solon climb wearily out of the trees, Raffi wondered where Carys was, in what fog of nightmare. And under it all ran his old terror of the Watch, the clang of the prison door, the agony of tiny worms burrowing into the flesh . . . he shuddered, so that Galen turned.

"Raffi?" he said. "Come and see this."

Raffi walked up to the brow of the hill, and stared down.

23

*"In fact, we have no rulers as such. The
Council of Seven are called the Karamax;
each member is chosen by its tribe. They
stay aloof from the Starmen. We find an
air of mystery can be useful to baffle the
curious. We have worked hard to make
the Watch take no account of us."*

Words of a Sekoi Karamax.
Recorded by Kallebran.

BELOW THEM LAY AN ENORMOUS CAMP. It was vast; a town pitched in a hollow, made of thousands of tents and pavilions and awnings and rickety booths, all shapes and colors, the small red fires brilliant in the cloudy glimmer of four moons.

The Sekoi stopped and folded its arms.

"There must be millions here!" Solon stared down in consternation. "Surely all your tribes? This is like a migration."

"Almost all." The slits in the creature's eyes were black and narrow. It turned. "Now listen to me, keepers. I've brought you here because the Watch must be shaken off

and because my people may know something to help our
search. I cannot promise that, but it may be." It smiled
complacently. "So I will do all the speaking here. You,
Galen, would be far too impatient. And your sense-lines,
I think, will not help you."

They knew that already. Of all the great host in front
of them, Raffi had not the ghost of a feeling. The sense-
lines told him the land was empty. It was a terrible decep-
tion. It made him feel blind.

Galen nodded, tying his black hair back. "You know
best. But we should hurry."

They scrambled down among the outlying booths.
Sekoi of all colors wandered out to stare at them, tall
and starved-looking in the flame light and shadows, the
silken gaudy fabrics of their tents flapping in the wind.
As they threaded deeper into the vast encampment, Raffi
wondered where the children were. You never saw any.
The Sekoi hid them as carefully as their gold.

Awnings rose above them now; great rippling hangings of precious satins brilliantly colored, gold and turquoise and purple. In front of each tent was a tall pole,
painted with stripes and odd angular signs that might

The Circling

be letters, running downwards. Bells hung here and there, chiming softly as the wind stirred them. Above all there were the owls, hundreds of them; gray owls and long-eared, ice-owls and three-toed—even ink-owls, perched everywhere, on tent pegs, on wooden rails, or just swooping in out of the dark, silent as moths under the tassels and silks.

The Sekoi walked ahead and Galen followed, nearly as tall, his dark coat making him a gaunt shadow among the fires. The camp smelled of trodden grass and smoke. It was crowded but strangely quiet. Solon looked around at the watching faces in avid curiosity, but Marco seemed oddly intimidated; he carried his crossbow, even unloaded, as if it were some comfort.

"Are you sure this isn't some sort of trap?" he muttered, glancing back.

Solon smiled kindly at him. "Nervous, my son?"

"Holiness, I'm scared stiff. There are thousands of them."

"They want nothing from us."

"Gold." Marco nursed the bow. "They'd do anything for gold. Mind you"—he grinned at Raffi—"so would I."

Raffi didn't smile. "So how much will you get for the Coronet?" he asked sourly.

Marco stared, his grin fading. After a moment he said, "That was hard, Raffi. You're getting like your master."

Raffi felt a flicker of shame. Until he remembered Carys. "She's not the spy," he said sullenly. "So who's left?"

The bald man had no time to retort. They had come to an enormous pavilion, the biggest structure in the maze of silks by far. It was made of some deep crimson fabric, and all its sides hung in elaborate folded shapes, rising to three high pinnacles where owls perched silent under rippling pennants.

The Sekoi turned. "Leave everything outside. Especially that bow."

Galen tossed the stick and pack down. Raffi did the same. Marco looked distinctly rebellious.

"Come on, old friend," Solon murmured. "No one will threaten us."

"You'd better be right." Marco dumped the bow ungraciously. "This lot scare me more than the Watch."

Galen glared at him darkly. "Maybe you should stay

The Circling

outside." It was the first time he had spoken to Marco since the observatory.

The bald man shook his head. "Oh no. You don't lose me that easily."

The Sekoi gave an impatient mew. "We're late. This way." It led them inside.

The first thing that struck Raffi was the scent. It was so sweet, a delicious sweetness of honey or sugared cakes. They walked on luxurious woven rugs and soft carpets that silenced their tread. Around them the walls and high ceiling rippled crimson. Small lamps sputtered on bronze stands; on a rail in the very center of the room an ancient gray owl slumbered, one eye slitted to watch them come.

"No one here," Marco whispered.

"Yes there is." The Sekoi said something to the owl in the Tongue. It hooted, long and low, and with a speed that startled Raffi, its wings opened and it swooped soundlessly out through an opening in the roof.

"Sit down," the Sekoi said graciously.

There were cushions, thick and glossy. Solon sank among them in relief. "What luxury. And what happens now?"

"Food." The Sekoi winked at Raffi. "We're a hospitable race."

When it came it was fruit, as he'd known it would be, but huge bowls of it, carried by an immensely strong Sekoi with pure white fur, its eyes amber and curious. Raffi was too hungry to wait; he ate berries and apples and the delicious soft flesh of the mavros eagerly, and drank the pale sherbet waters with Solon, debating about which was the best. Galen picked at the fruit, watching Marco, who said nothing and prowled uneasily.

Until the Karamax walked in.

There were seven of them, all tall and all masked. The masks were elaborate, covering the upper half of the face, made of satin and adorned with bizarre slashes of gold, with feathers and strange painted symbols. The eyes of the creatures behind them were amber and gold.

Galen went to move but the Sekoi glared at him and stood up, a tall, elegant figure. It began to speak urgently in the Tongue, its long fingers gesturing, and the seven Karamax sat on the cushions listening, their eyes flickering to the Starmen.

It bothered Raffi that he could feel nothing of them. He

The Circling

had grown to depend on the awen-field more than he'd realized.

The story took a long time. Finally the Sekoi fell silent. The Karamax gazed at each other. Then the tallest, a red-furred creature dressed in yellow and blue, stood up. Its voice was female, and it spoke so they could all understand. "We have relived this tale with interest. We welcome you, keepers, and share our sorrows for your losses. Your enemies are our enemies. However, I fear there is little we can do except give you shelter. This relic our friend speaks of is unknown to us and we have no interest in such devices. The Makers' power we acknowledge freely, but they are not our Makers . . ."

Galen leaped up, irritated. "Are you sure?" His voice was bitter with disappointment.

The Sekoi waved him back, alarmed. The Karamax seemed to stiffen.

"We have had this argument before," the red-furred one said gently. "The Makers . . ."

Galen waved impatiently. "Not that! Are you sure you know nothing of the Coronet? Surely, in one of your many stories . . ."

"Nothing."

Solon was on his feet too. "This is bitterly disappointing for us."

"I know it. And for us too the weather is a cause of much disquiet," the Karamax said smoothly, "but . . ." It stopped.

Outside the door-curtain loud voices were raised, one insistent, others angry. Suddenly the curtain was twitched aside, and two huge Sekoi marched in. Between them, struggling and furious, was a girl with soaked hair, the red dye almost washed out of it.

"Carys!" Raffi leaped up in delight.

The Sekoi gave a snarl of wrath. "You!"

"Yes, me!" She grinned at it, triumphant. "I told you no cage would hold me. I suppose they've already given you their excuses, Galen? Tried to fob you off with a pack of lies?"

He came forward and caught her arm. "What are you talking about, Carys?"

She laughed, scornful, shaking free of the sentinels. "Don't you see? The Coronet is gold, isn't it? Gold! So they've got it. It's part of their Great Hoard, Galen, prob-

The Circling

ably the most precious part. The Sekoi have the Coronet.
They've had it for centuries."

Astonished, he stared at her. "How do you know?"

She had looked forward to this. She drew herself up
and grinned at him, enjoying it.

"Flain told me," she said.

24

*In the night the innkeeper crept into
her room. The purse lay on a table;
stealthily he opened it. One gold coin
fell out. Then another. And another. The
innkeeper capered with delight. He ran
down the stairs and called to his wife.
"We're rich!" he cried. The gold kept
coming. More and more of it. And then
he knew he couldn't stop it.*

Agramon's Purse

SHE SHOULD HAVE KNOWN he wouldn't be surprised. For a moment he almost smiled at her.

Then he gave the Sekoi a sharp look. "Is it true?"

The creature made a mew of disgust. "Of course it's not true! I would have told you at the beginning!"

"You might not have known." Dangerously tense, Galen turned on the Council of Seven. "Tell me the truth," he said. "I ask you in the name of Flain and all your own secret gods. Do you have the Coronet?"

The seven Karamax exchanged glances. Behind their masks their eyes were sharp and uneasy. Finally one of them shrugged.

"All right. We do."

The silence in the tent was immense; it was the Sekoi who broke it. It snarled angrily in the Tongue, all the fur on its neck swelling with rage.

The Karamax spoke back, rapidly, three of them, but the Sekoi flung away, disgusted. "Galen," it snapped, "I swear to you I had no knowledge of this. None!"

"Liar," Carys said calmly. She folded her arms. "Admit it. You knew the whole time. And this Watchspy business. There *is* someone else who knew about the Crow. It's *you*!"

"Stop it." Galen's eyes were black. "We don't have time. The Coronet is what we're here for."

He watched the seven closely. "You must let us use it. I swear we won't try to take it from you. You say our enemies are yours—then work with us. Help us!"

A Karamax with gray fur and a black and gold mask shook its head. "Unthinkable. We don't know your reasons."

"Indeed," the red-furred female said kindly. "You must plead your case. On the strength of it we will make our decision. And it will be final. Agreed?"

The Circling

Galen turned. "Well?"

The Sekoi shrugged angrily. "You've got no choice."

"Solon?"

"Yes, my son. And I will speak."

Galen turned back. "Agreed," he said heavily.

The sentinels went back to the door. Carys pushed past Marco and sat by Raffi. She poured out blue sherbet water. "Glad to see me?"

"What happened to you?" he whispered.

She drank thirstily. "Tell you later. I want to hear this."

Only Solon was standing now. Around him the red tent rippled and flapped in the rising wind; before him on silk cushions the Karamax sat, eyes bright in the slits of their masks. The gray owl flew soundlessly onto its perch. It preened out one downy feather that drifted to the floor.

Solon seemed uncertain how begin. "Friends," he said at last. "You've heard our story. Our search for this relic has been a strange one, and time is running out. The Makers have told us that the Coronet is a device that will stabilize something they called the weather-net. It will also, we hope, arrest the movement of the moon Agramon."

The Council eyed one another.

Marco shifted, restless. "Come on, old friend," he breathed.

Solon licked dry lips. He gave his kindest smile. "Believe me, we understand that gold is precious to you. But this relic is small. It weighs little. And because it was Flain's, that makes it the property of his successors, that is, the Order. I am Solon, Archkeeper of the Order. I am the last successor of Flain."

Marco's eyebrows shot up. He looked at Raffi. Raffi nodded, silent.

"The weather is decaying," Solon went on, holding his hands out. "Anara is dying. From all sides come reports of hurricanes, floods, destruction. Whole populations of birds and animals swarm and panic. We will all be killed if it worsens, both Sekoi and Starmen. I beg you to listen to us. We are not the Watch, my friends; we want only what is good for us all. Too many have suffered already; we have seen men and women injured and weeping over their children's bodies. Soon more will be homeless; there will be famine and disease. For Flain's sake, for all our sakes, let us use the Coronet. It is little enough to ask. You are a gentle race. I know you will help us."

The Circling

He sounded so wise and anxious that Raffi felt a great hope. They could never turn him down.

Solon let his hands fall.

The red-furred Karamax stood and looked at the owl. One eye open, the owl looked back. The crimson walls rippled, rain pattering on them.

The Karamax cleared its throat. "Thank you, Archkeeper," it said softly. "We are saddened at your distress. We see the marks of the pain you have suffered. Because of that, we have decided to tell you things here that few others of your kind will ever have heard." To their surprise it reached up and took its mask off, and they saw a young female, with a tribemark under one ear. "First, your claim as successor of Flain. We cannot admit this as a factor. The Sekoi own the Coronet now, we have had it for centuries. We have no laws of inheritance or restitution."

The Sekoi sighed, and shook its head.

"Secondly, the weather. This decay has long been predicted."

"By whom?" Solon asked, startled.

"You are not the only ones with sacred stories." It

smiled slyly. "My people know the Makers will return. Before they come, many evil portents will occur. It is said that the sky will darken and the moons, one by one, will fall from the sky. The land will shake and the things of Kest, even the Margrave himself, will be destroyed. The planet will be cleansed. This is what has started to happen. We do not wish to interfere."

"Then you must be alarmed . . ."

"Not at all. For we are ready. The Sekoi will not be touched by this disaster. We have . . . places. Secure places, deep underground. Here we will wait until it is safe to emerge. This is the reason for our gathering. Soon every Sekoi will vanish from Anara, and no Starman will know where we have gone."

Except me, Carys thought idly. But no, the Palace of Theriss would have a fit if it had to accommodate all these. She wondered just how many secrets the Sekoi had. The Watch had underestimated them all these years.

"What about us?" Marco demanded. "The rest of us?"

The red-furred Sekoi looked at him. "We do not know. Maybe your Makers will come in time to save you."

The Circling

"I don't believe in the Makers."

The Karamax blinked. "Then you are a fool," it said quietly.

Marco looked so astonished that Raffi almost smiled.

"So you will let the world be ruined?" Solon was appalled. "Allow hundreds of people to be killed?"

"It has been foretold. The Coronet is only a circle of gold. It can do nothing to stop the decay."

"But it can!" Galen couldn't keep silent any longer. He leaped up, the shadow of the Crow crackling around him. Side by side with Solon he faced them. "We know it can! Surely your obsessed lust for gold is . . ."

"You do not understand." The Karamax pointed. "Your friend there. He understands."

The Sekoi was huddled miserably among the cushions, gnawing at its nails. It gave Galen a bitter look. "It's no use. They won't give it up."

Galen spun back. "Explain. Tell us!"

"It concerns the Great Hoard."

Immediately the owl made a small chirring noise. The female Karamax went to it and spoke, then stroked its plumage. "For hundreds of years my people have collected gold. Your Order and the Watch have always wondered where it went. Some thieves"—its glance flickered to Marco—"have even tried to find it. No one ever has. The purpose of the Hoard is a hidden one, but because you are the Crow, Galen Harn, and this is the end of the age, I will tell you what it is."

It stepped away from the owl, slipped its mask back on, and moved to the center of the Seven, sitting complacently on the silk cushions.

"The purpose of the Hoard is to buy Anara."

Outside, the wind gave a great roar. The canvas billowed, slapping against its ropes and pegs. Raffi's senselines swung with it, dizzying, a huge aftershock.

"Buy?" Solon whispered.

Galen's stare was dark and even. "From the Makers!" he said.

"Exactly." Another of the Karamax was speaking now. "The world was ours once. When the Makers return, it will be cleansed, and we will ransom it with an enormous treasure."

Solon looked at Galen. He seemed too astonished to speak. Finally he plunged his hands through his silver

The Circling

hair. "You really believe this? That the Makers will . . . sell the world?"

"Yes."

"But you have no idea . . ."

"And you have never seen the Great Hoard." Behind its mask the creature's eyes were bright with greed. "It holds more riches, keeper, than you could ever imagine. It will buy the Sekoi their world back. And every fragment of it, every ring, every coin, every little gold circle, will be needed." It looked at the other six, who nodded. "The Coronet will not be given up. That is our decision."

"No!" Solon threw his arms out. "Those who die . . . !"

"Must die."

The wind screamed. For a moment Raffi thought Solon would fling himself to his knees in complete despair but Galen gripped him gently and turned him, small energies rippling around his hands.

He looked down at Raffi and Carys.

There was nothing left to say.

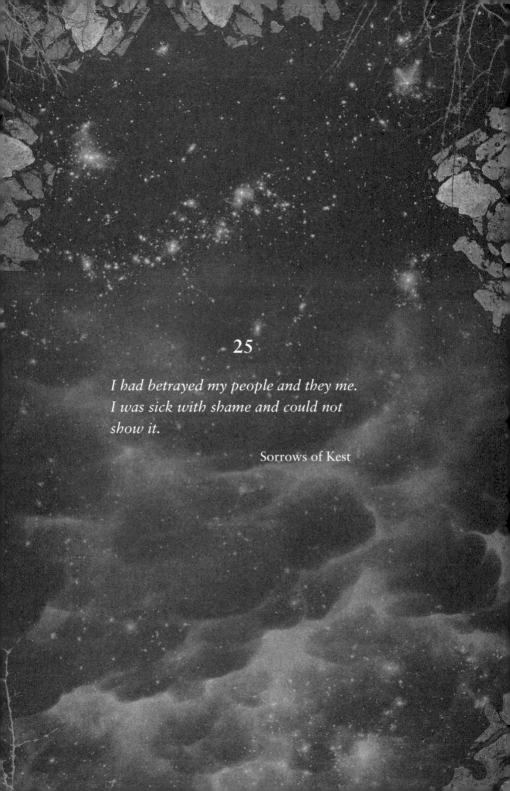

25

*I had betrayed my people and they me.
I was sick with shame and could not
show it.*

Sorrows of Kest

THEY WERE GIVEN A SMALL TENT but none of them could sleep.

Outside, another squall raged, sleeting in through the entrance, hissing out the fire. It was Solon who seemed most devastated by events; the Archkeeper usually cheered everyone up, made small teasing jokes, but he was drawn and white now, as if some great pain had struck him. And the Sekoi had gone, stalking off into the rain.

Galen took down the lamp, spread the awen-beads carefully around it, and began the Litany. His voice was grave but even, and the familiar Maker-words seemed slowly to take some chill out of their hearts and the damp night. Raffi joined in, and after a while Solon murmured the responses, as if he clutched at them for comfort.

Carys sat in a corner, watching. Marco cleaned and loaded his crossbow.

When the prayer was over, the silence seemed worse, until the curtain was whipped back and the Sekoi ducked in.

They stared at it. It was drenched, its brindled gray fur dark and sopping, water trickling down its neck and sleeves.

"Galen, I'm sorry," it said, its voice strangled.

"Not your fault." The Relic Master stood, his dark hair brushing the tent roof. He smiled sourly. "I told you a long time ago I knew the Sekoi had their own ways."

"I didn't know we had it! I swear!"

Raffi had never seen the creature look so wretched. It crumpled and sat, arms around knees. All its airy confidence had been knocked right out of it; it even looked thinner, its fur scraggy.

The Circling

Galen sat beside it, his hooked face half in shadow.

"I believe you," he said softly. "But do you think too that all Starmen should be left to die?"

The creature dragged in a breath. When it spoke its voice was reluctant. "We've always been taught so. Most of us are not interested in the fate of Starmen." It looked up. "Neither was I, once."

"And now?"

It gave an exasperated hiss. "Don't torment me. You know I would help you if I could. But . . ."

"You can. Take us to the Great Hoard."

Raffi drew his breath in. The Sekoi sat quite still. Small raindrops dripped from its fur. Then it said, "I knew you would ask this."

"But you still came back." Galen caught hold of its arm. Blue sparks flickered from his fingers. "If we don't use the Coronet the weather will overwhelm us all. The Makers will find no one alive. And even if the Sekoi survive, what use is a ruined world?"

The creature pulled away, utterly miserable. "You don't know what you're asking. I can't."

"We need you," Solon pleaded. "Please!"

"It's against all I believe in!" The creature's voice was agonized, its eyes dark slits. "How can I take outsiders to the Hoard? How can I take a thief and a spy and three keepers to our most holy place? You're asking too much, Galen!"

The Relic Master sat still, though his shadow swung as the lamp moved. Raffi felt the power of the Crow pent up inside him, the tingle of it on the skin.

"But that's what we did." Galen's voice was harsh. "We took you to Sarres. The spy and the thief and the Sekoi. We trusted you."

The Sekoi winced. "Don't ask me."

"But I do ask you." Suddenly Galen had both of its wrists tight; the crackle of energy sparked up around all of them. Marco yelped. Raffi sat breathless with tension. "Take us there! We'll take nothing! But we must hurry. We must go now!"

For a long moment the Sekoi was still. It closed its eyes in something like despair.

Then it pushed him away, stood up, and brushed the water from its fur with both long hands.

"I make myself an outcast by this," it muttered.

362

The Circling

❄❄❄

THEY RAN THROUGH THE CAMP, stumbling in the raging squall. Above them the awnings were wild screaming flickers, torn and frayed. All the owls were gone, every Sekoi undercover, and that was their only chance, Raffi thought, his sense-lines swept away. He crashed against Carys, who hissed with annoyance.

The noise was incredible. Ducking under sodden hangings, the Sekoi led them swiftly, Galen with Solon close behind, Marco last, watching their backs, bow firmly braced. Carys glanced at it enviously. "We should have found mine!" she screamed in Raffi's ear.

Purple silk plastered against his face; he tore it off. "No time!"

The roar of the storm covered them; it was a weight, a lid of blackness lit with low flickers of lightning.

At the camp's edge the Sekoi paused. "Run now!" it yelled.

They were in the open. They raced into darkness between the last tents, stumbling over tussocky grass, fleeing the relentless deafening flap of silk, climbing hard, up and up as if into the storm-cloud. Breathless and soaked, Raffi slipped, grabbing handfuls of wet grass. At the top they glanced back. In a glimmer of lightning the camp was there and then gone.

The Sekoi stared down at it, face drenched and blank. Solon patted it kindly on the shoulder. "All will be well, my friend."

The Sekoi looked past him at Carys. "Will it?" it said coldly.

For an hour they hurried through the storm. Galen was relentless and would allow few rests, but even Solon was anxious to keep going.

"How far is this place?" Marco gasped as they crashed down through a sheshorn copse.

The Sekoi glared. "Never mind."

Marco laughed, hefting the bow. "Scared I'll find my way back one day?"

"My son, there may not be many more days if we fail," Solon muttered, stumbling. The bald man grabbed him. "Keep your feet, Holiness."

Carys turned, looking for Raffi. He was far behind; she waited, anxious. "Are you all right?"

The Circling

"Yes."

But he wasn't. It had come again, that flicker of evil. Something dark, right among them. Something he had seen once before, a shape that still lurked at the back of his mind, in the corners of his nightmares.

Carys looked at him hard, then said, "Tell me later. Come on."

The storm faded. After a while there was only rain and wind and then even the rain died, and above the trees they saw patches of sky glinting with stars. They ran down steep, rutted tracks hollowed by the passage of a thousand Sekoi-carts. It was hard to keep their footing in the puddles and mud; Galen slipped on his stiff leg and swore. Splashing through a stream they plunged back into a fir wood, the trunks so black and closely set that even the Sekoi lost its way and only Galen's hurried conversation with the trees got them out.

An hour later, as they climbed a steep hillside, the moons came out, all seven, with Lar very low to the east. Raffi gazed up at them in relief, but Carys grabbed his coat.

"What's that?"

On the ridge above them a vast dim shape rose against

the stars. It was crouching down, and for a second Raffi thought it some monster of Maar, gigantic and watchful, one arm flung out, until the sense-lines told him it had no life. It was stone.

"Climb up to it," the Sekoi muttered.

They pulled themselves up wearily, under the colossus. In the darkness its dim eyes seemed to watch them come, a vast kneeling Sekoi, crowned with silver, its hand pointing away over the hilltop.

In its shadow they paused for breath. Marco stared up in amazement. "So there were cat-kings, once." He moved out of the Sekoi's hearing and said quietly, "Can you credit their crazy ideas? To buy the planet! How can they believe that?"

"Faith is not about reason," Solon said gravely. "It's another thing altogether."

"I wouldn't know."

Solon rubbed his muddy hands in distress. "My son, you may surprise us all yet."

Galen was looking back; beside him Raffi knew he was sensing deep into soil and stone.

"Are they coming?"

The Circling

"Not yet."

"But you can't feel the Sekoi," Carys said.

"I can feel any disturbance of the trees. There's none as yet."

She looked around. "We ought to set up a few traps. Slow them down."

Galen smiled, mirthless. "Training dies hard, Carys. Let them come."

"Even the Watch?" Seeing his look, she moved closer, her voice low. "I ran into them, a patrol, back at the observatory. They're following us. Someone's getting information straight to Maar, Galen, and I don't understand who or how."

He was still a moment. Then he said, "I know."

The path led right under the cat-king's body, a trail beaten around its vast knee and over a half-buried foot. Marco watched the serene face nervously, all the way.

Over the hill the land dropped. Now they could see other colossi spaced out over a wide plain, some sitting, some standing like grim sentinels, each pointing the way to an immense and bizarre ruin far off on the horizon, a dark outline that troubled Raffi's nerves.

Slowly, the moons climbed above them. At their fastest pace it took over two hours to cross the plain, and as they came to the last statue the Sekoi stopped and doubled up, clutching its side.

"Need a rest," it gasped.

Marco already had his boot off and was rubbing a sore foot; Carys and Solon drank from the water flasks. Unwinding the scarf from his neck Raffi shuddered, and stopped.

Snow had begun to fall. Through it he saw at last the image of the Margrave. It loomed out of his memory, a hateful shadowy outline turning toward him, its dry reptilian whisper mocking him.

"Raffi."

He couldn't move. He was sweating, felt utterly sick.

"Raffi?" Galen caught his arm. "What is it?"

Dazed, he looked around. Snow fell between them. Galen's voice was oddly quiet. "What did you see?"

He moistened dry lips. "Him. The Margrave."

Galen crouched. "Are you sure?"

"Of course I'm sure!"

"Keep your voice down."

The Circling

Raffi rubbed his face anxiously with both hands. Then he whispered. "It's here, isn't it? With us?"

"Galen?" The Sekoi's tall shadow darkened them. "We must hurry."

It stood aside, and in the drift of the snow they saw a host of bell-like shapes, each hanging from a wooden pole.

"What's this?" Marco asked gruffly. "More trouble?"

"Shadowchimes." The Sekoi shrugged gracefully. "As our shadows touch them they will chime out a warning. I'm afraid there is nothing we can do about it. My people will know."

"It doesn't matter anyway." Galen looked back over the plain.

Carys crossed to him. "They're coming?"

"Hundreds of them. Fast."

"How long have we got?"

"I don't know." He looked at the Sekoi. "Are we close?"

The creature turned and walked into the chimefield.

"We're here," it said.

The Great Hoard

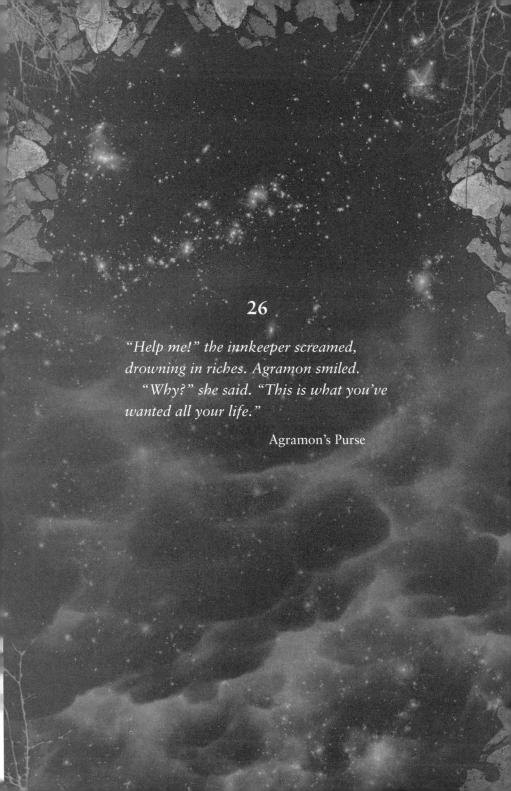

26

*"Help me!" the innkeeper screamed,
drowning in riches. Agramon smiled.
     "Why?" she said. "This is what you've
wanted all your life."*

Agramon's Purse

THEY WERE UNDER THE WALLS of the ruin. Behind them the shadowchimes still rang; gong-like notes, soft and disturbing.

Raffi put a hand on the wall, feeling through the holes in his gloves how each enormous block of stone had been expertly fitted, though now snarlbines and weeds were sprouting through the cracks.

Snow clung to his hair; strange wet stuff, faintly phosphorescent. He climbed hurriedly after Galen, up steep steps and under a vast drafty archway into a dark interior. The floor was paved here; all around were arches and galleries, the stonework fallen and crumbling, making their footsteps echo and multiply like some invading army.

It was bitterly cold.

As he came through, small shadows slunk behind him; turning, he saw their eyes gleam in the dark. The sense-lines told him they were cats, cats of all sizes and colors, their pointed inquisitive faces alert in holes and on walls.

The Sekoi climbed ahead, a spindly figure. As it emerged into the open again, snow clotted its fur.

"There," it said proudly. "What no Starman ever beheld until now. The Great Hoard."

Below them a huge arena descended, a ghostly crater of stone. Thousands of seats and steps and galleries gleamed pale in the snow-light, and out of them sprouted a jungle of weeds and self-seeded plants, in places tangled into tunnels of gloom. A sweet smell of mutated flowers rose up from its depths; they saw white frostblossoms and tiny spring bulbs that had thrust out and flowered already in the drafty shelter of columns and balustrades, and from the split seating bulbous fungi ballooned.

Clouds drifted; a few stars gleamed. Agramon lit a sudden cascade of snow. And everywhere, they saw the gold.

It was scattered freely down the stairs, piled and heaped, barrows and cart-loads and buckets of it; there were boxes and chests and crates that had broken so that the heavy coins had slid and tinkled out. Some had been there so long scarbines had crawled all over them, roots cracking through split wood. Raffi saw plates, dishes, candlesticks, jewelry, goblets, mangled scraps of gilt, broken relics, statues, rings; anything that could be stolen or won or bought was down there, spilling in shining rivers down the stairways into a heap so enormous that it looked from here like a hill of gold.

They were silent, their breath clouding the frosty air.

Then Marco managed a pale grin. "Flainsteeth," he said. "It must have taken decades."

"Centuries." The Sekoi stroked an eyebrow. "Since the Makers left."

"There must be millions. Billions . . ."

Solon smiled gently. "No wonder your people feel confident of their ransom. But how are we to find the Coronet in all this?"

"I have only been here once before." The creature

brushed snow from its fur. All at once it looked nervous. "I suspect your relic will be in the center, on . . ." It stopped, then turned.

"Galen, listen. Only the Karamax are allowed down there, into the heart of the Hoard. I will take you, and the Archkeeper, for the sake of our friendship and because I believe your quest for the relic is a true one, though if my people find us there, it is likely we will all die."

Galen nodded, his eyes dark. "You won't be sorry."

"I am already sorry. The others—even the small keeper—must remain up here. They have already come too far."

Its yellow eyes looked at him sharply. Galen nodded. "I agree."

"Well, I don't," Carys muttered.

Galen turned to her urgently. "We must respect their beliefs." But his mind was saying something else, and to her amazement she could hear it, something that made her clench her fingers on the cold spangles of snow. She nodded, reluctant. "If you say so."

Marco sat himself down.

The Great Hoard

"And you," Solon said to him severely, "will not let your fingers stray to the tiniest edge of the least coin."

"Holiness! What do you take me for?"

"A thief and a rogue, my son."

Marco grinned. "And I thought I'd fooled you all along."

Galen dumped the pack and hauled out his stick. He looked at Raffi. "When they come, keep them out as long as you can. Use the awen-field, use the third and even the fourth Actions. I don't want anyone killed, but we must have time to find the relic."

Chilled to the heart, Raffi nodded. "Understood."

Galen glanced at Carys. "I'm depending on you."

She smiled wryly. "Good luck."

Then he and Solon and the Sekoi were gone, ducking under an archway into darkness.

IT ALL SEEMED SUDDENLY QUIET.

Raffi crouched out of the snow. He felt sick with bitter disappointment. All this way. And now he would never even see the Coronet.

Marco put the crossbow down and hugged himself. "God, it's cold. We should get a fire going."

But no one moved. They huddled in silence. Far below, something slithered, a distant clatter of movement. The fall of the snow around them was almost hypnotic, and through it Raffi could feel the cats gathering, a stealthy curiosity in the shadows. When the moons glimmered out, he saw their eyes, hundreds of them, pale green and amber.

Marco looked around. "Shoo," he said.

The cats scattered.

Instantly Carys reached out, grabbed the crossbow, and aimed it at his head. The bald man froze in mid-scramble.

"God almighty," he muttered. "Be careful!"

"I'm very careful. Sit down."

Inch by inch, he sank back. His face looked tauter, older. "So you really are the spy," he said icily.

"No." Her eyes were steady. "You are."

"That's absolute rubbish."

"Galen thinks so. He thought you'd try and follow him. Asked me to stop you." She leaned a little closer. "Tell me this, Marco, how did you manage it? I can't work that out. How did you get the messages back?"

He shook his head, then froze as the bow twitched. "It's not me." He glanced at Raffi. "You don't think so, do you? I'm a thief, yes, and a liar, but a spy? Never. Not for the Watch. Not after I've hung in their stinking prisons."

Raffi was shivering. He was almost too confused to think, but after a moment he said, "Someone is. Someone has the Margrave inside them."

They stared at him, horrified.

"Inside?" Carys breathed.

He wrapped his arms tight around himself, rocking slightly, not looking at her. She thought he seemed on the edge of some nightmare; his voice had a harsh, broken strain.

"All the way here I've sensed it. Small things at first. Cold touches. As we've gone on, it's gotten stronger. As if I'm tuning in."

"But the Margrave!" Carys's whisper scattered the returning cats.

"I saw him once, remember? Since then I've felt . . . as if he knows me." He looked up. "We're not the only ones looking for the Coronet. He's using us to find it for him. One of us, whether we know it or not, is telling him everything. He's so deep inside one of our minds that even Galen can't find him."

They were silent. Then Marco said, "Unless Galen is the spy himself."

SOLON SLIPPED; the Sekoi grabbed him quickly. A glissade of coins slithered underfoot, an avalanche of tiny shining circles, catching the moons.

It had been hard to find a way down. They had to thread a maze of aisles and galleries, stoop through tunnels of ancient mirrorwort. Down here it was darker, and the snow was beginning to freeze, crunching underfoot and making the hoard glimmer with weird light. Gold was a landscape around them; Galen glanced up at the towering mountains of it, the hills and valleys, whole revenues of treasure, cold and shining.

"What a fortune it is," Solon marveled.

Galen snorted. "And how many hungry bellies it could feed."

The Great Hoard

The Sekoi paused. "I think this path may be the one."
But it still seemed hesitant. Then it turned abruptly. "I
have to ask you one more thing."

"What?" Galen said, wary.

The creature's eyes were evasive. "There is something . . . unusual at the heart of the Hoard. Something
that will amaze you." It bit its thumbnail. "Keepers, I
want you to swear you will never tell anyone what you
see."

"AH, BUT THIS CROW THING!" Marco ignored
Raffi's anger. "I mean, what is it? What can it make
him do? You don't really know anything about it, do
you?"

"It's a gift from the Makers!"

"Ha! So was the Margrave!"

"It can't be Galen!" Raffi was white with fury. "It's
impossible!"

"Calm down!" Carys said quietly. "When have you
sensed these warnings? Try to remember. Exactly when?"

He held his head in both hands. "By the river. At the

Circling. Just outside here—it was certain then. And in the vortex. That night in the cellar."

The bow flickered; Carys glanced at him for one startled instant.

At once Marco's foot shot out; he slammed her back against the wall and she screamed in fury. The bolt splintered stone and suddenly they were both struggling for the bow, Raffi leaping up in horror, until Carys was shoved away and Marco had the bow under one arm and his knife hard against her neck.

"See how you like it," he growled.

Carys dragged muddy hair from her face. She looked white and breathless, but her voice was concentrated with suppressed excitement.

"Neither of us was in the cellar," she said.

THE PATH WAS A TRAIL OF GOLD. Coins had been trodden deep in the mud, one on another. On each side rose a hillock of spilling metal, and as the moons drifted through the snow-cloud Galen saw in the very heart of the Hoard a great golden reliquary, carved and encrusted

The Great Hoard

with gems. It stood on a platform; the Sekoi led them up to it without a word, and under the moons each of them had seven shadows, a hidden company that seemed to follow stealthily at their heels.

Solon's scarred fingers reached for the handrail; above him the Sekoi reached down to help. Galen hauled himself after them, the snow falling in his eyes. At the top the Archkeeper stared, then crumpled to his knees.

"Dear God," was all he could say.

The reliquary was a coffin, sealed with glass.

In it lay a man.

A small man, thin and wiry. He had brown hair and a clipped brown beard and his clothes were of Makercloth, incorruptible and perfect. He had been dead for three hundred years, but he looked as if at any second he might open his eyes and speak to them.

Galen stood still, catching his breath as if struck with a sharp pain.

At the heart of the Great Hoard they had found the body of Kest.

And Flain's Coronet lay between his hands.

27

Each man on this world has seven shadows.

Poems of Anjar Kar

THEY BOTH STARED AT HER.

"Think about it!" Ignoring the knife, Carys turned on Raffi. "Marco was on the next street! I was miles away. So was the Sekoi. The only ones in the cellar with you were Solon and Galen! It has to be one of them!"

"Not Galen!" Raffi snapped.

"And not Solon!" Marco lowered the knife. He looked stunned and winded, as if someone had punched him in the stomach. "They tortured him. I saw them drag him back into the cell. I saw him bleed. They were going to hang us."

"No, they weren't!" Carys shook her head, impatient.

"It was a setup, all of it. Solon was the bait—they wanted him to be rescued. Work it out!" She looked at his face and her voice softened. "Marco, the Margrave must have heard the rumors about the Crow—they'd be in every intelligence return. So they set up bait—a keeper, someone whose mind is so broken they can control him. Maybe more than one, in different places. Public places, where everyone can see. And when Galen rescued Solon, the Margrave let it happen. We took the Margrave with us, to all our places. To Sarres. To the Great Hoard." She shook her head desperately. "We were so stupid! It's the oldest trick in the book. And because Solon was such a harmless, kindly old man . . ."

"No!" Marco twisted away.

She grabbed his sleeve. "Believe it. It's true. I know how they work."

"Not Solon." His voice was an agony. Raffi looked away, feeling sick and miserable, but Carys was relentless. "Solon! And we've led him straight to the Coronet."

"He wouldn't."

"He's down there, isn't he? And if he puts it on . . ." She whirled on Raffi, her face white in the falling snow.

The Great Hoard

"My God, Raffi! If he puts it on, the Margrave will control the weather-net, the moons, who knows what! We may have given him the greatest weapon in the world."

IT WAS A CIRCLE OF DULL GOLD, frail and perfect. On the inside were minute letters, strange and unreadable. Galen reached out and brushed the scattered snow off the glass. "So this is your ransom," he whispered.

The Sekoi was staring at the dead face of the Maker. "Indeed. I had always known he was here, but how strange it is to see him. The one who caused all our anguish. Who ruined a world, and then repented."

"How did he come here?"

The Sekoi shrugged. "I'm not of the Council. They might know. Alone of the Makers only Kest truly died. When the others had gone my people must have brought his body here. But I know nothing of how, or from where."

Solon had not moved. When he uncovered his face they caught the wet glint of tears. Galen bent over him. "Come," he said gruffly. "We need to hurry."

But the Archkeeper seemed struck to the heart. His astonishment was deeply personal, a grief that Galen felt rising from somewhere endlessly deep inside him, a great pit, a terrible darkness.

"After all this time," he muttered. "To see him again."

He bowed his head, then staggered up unsteadily and looked around. For a second he seemed hardly to know where he was.

"All right?" Galen asked.

"Yes, my son." The Archkeeper wiped his face with his sleeve. "The shock."

"We need to open the glass." Galen put both hands on it and pushed, then sent a line of energy rippling around its edges feverishly.

"How does it work?"

The Sekoi bit its nails. "I don't know."

"I'll break it if I have to," Galen growled. But to his astonishment he felt the glass melt. Suddenly there was no lid. Tiny flakes of snow fluttered onto Kest's hair.

"Take it," Solon whispered. "Hurry!"

They were each filled with the same thought, that Kest would open his eyes, snatch Galen's hand. With

The Great Hoard

an effort Galen reached down and touched the Maker's hands.

They were cold, and as he lifted the Coronet from them carefully he thought that these were the hands that had made evil, that had brought it into the world.

He shook the thought away and looked at the relic.

It was icy. Its very touch went through his mind like a silent chord of music, and it was light in his hands, as if it had no weight. Moonlight reflected from it. He held it on his palms; the precious, fragile hope of the world.

"What now?" The Sekoi fidgeted.

Galen was still. Then he held the Coronet out. "Archkeeper."

"My son, surely the Crow . . ."

"This is for you to do. The leader of the Order. Who better than a healer to heal the weather?"

Solon smiled ruefully. He nodded and held out his scarred hands. The moonlight touched the edge of his face and through the soft drift of falling snow his hair gleamed like silver. His fingers closed over Galen's.

"Don't let him take it!"

The yell rang across the vast arena. Echoes of it sent

loose fragments of stone crashing. The Sekoi jumped; Solon snatched the Coronet and whirled around.

"He's the spy! It's him!" Carys leaped down from the slithering gold, breathless and gasping. She aimed the bow hurriedly.

Behind them Marco dropped to the ground. In an instant he had rushed at them; Galen took a quick step back, then a flicker of light cracked from his hands. There was a stench of scorched flesh and Marco yelped, rolling in agony, the knife clattering onto the heap of treasure.

"You fool!" he yelled at Galen. "Don't you see?"

Galen turned, grim-faced.

Solon had the knife. He slashed the air with it. "Keep back," he snarled. "All of you!"

The change in him horrified them. It was a total transformation, something deep in the tissues of his skin, so that his eyes were darker and the very muscles of his face had clenched and hardened, all his kindliness dropped like a mask.

"Put the bow down."

Carys didn't waver. "If you try and put the relic on," she said tightly, "I'll kill you."

The Great Hoard

"I believe you." He smiled, a crooked, unfamiliar smile. "But your hands aren't your own now. Not if I want them to be mine. They have been mine a long time."

To her horror she felt her fingers slacken. The bow clattered among the gold, its bolt spilling out.

Solon raised the Coronet in one hand. "Now watch," he said.

Gold coins slithered; he whipped around in alarm, but Raffi's energy-line snagged him around the wrist; it crackled and spat and Raffi hurled himself after it, but Marco was faster. Grabbing the frail Coronet with his great fist he struggled chest to chest with the Archkeeper. In a swirl of snow they both held it, the awen-field crackling around them, but even as Galen ran forward Marco waved him back.

"It's me, Holiness! It's Marco!"

"Marco?" The Archkeeper's eyes flickered; for a second doubt came into them.

"You won't hurt me. Come on, Holiness, let me have the crown. We'll look after you."

Solon shook his head, bewildered.

"Oh, my old friend," he said. "I'm sorry." His arm

pulled back. He stabbed, driving the knife deep in under the ribs, vicious and hard.

Marco's breath croaked. He collapsed on hands and knees. In the moonlight his dark blood dripped on the snow, but Raffi had jerked the lines tight and suddenly out of the night the terrible wrath of the Crow swooped down on them all, a heaviness like beating wings; Solon was flung aside and lay crumpled on the treasure, the Coronet spilling from his hand, rolling over coins and cups to the Sekoi's feet, where it clattered and spun and lay still.

For a second none of them could move.

Then the Sekoi grabbed the relic and Galen was on his knees easing Marco over.

The bald man hissed with pain. Blood was everywhere; already it had soaked his jerkin and coat and stained the coins under him. Raffi knew there was nothing they could do.

Galen lifted his head gently. "Marco?"

The man's eyes opened. He forced a grin. "Sorry now, keeper?"

"What can I . . . ?"

The Great Hoard

"Save it. No time." He winced, turning his head to look at Solon in disbelief. "I loved that old man. But how he's used us. You and me. The girl and the creature. Set us up against each other; maybe even brought me along for it. Suspecting each other. Not him. He was laughing . . . behind our backs."

"It's not Solon," Galen said urgently. "It's the evil that rules him."

Marco nodded weakly. "But he let it. Let it in. I wouldn't have. Nor would you." His hand tightened on Galen's, then slid down to the coins, grasping a fistful. "Look at this. More than I've ever had in my life."

For a second he held them tight. Then his grip loosened, the money slithering away.

"What a joke," he whispered.

Snow settled on his still chest. Far and cold, Raffi felt the spark of his life go out, like a candle.

In utter silence, Galen made the sign of Flain on his forehead, palms, and chest. Raffi whispered some words of the Litany, but after only two lines the Sekoi crouched.

"Galen," it said anxiously. "They're here."

The keeper didn't move at once. He laid Marco down

and his face was as bleak as Raffi had ever seen it, as if he could barely control his devastation. Then he stood and looked up, as Carys was already doing.

All around, high on the ramparts of the arena, the Sekoi tribes were watching. Thousands of them stood up there, their eyes bright as cats' in the dark, the snow drifting silently onto their fur.

"Use it!" The Sekoi held the Coronet out as if the metal burned its hands. "Quickly!"

Galen was still. He was looking at Solon as the old man's eyes opened; instantly Carys raised the reloaded bow.

"No," the keeper whispered.

"Galen?"

Eyes black with loss, Galen turned. "No. You do it."

The Sekoi blinked. "Me?"

"You and your people."

"But . . ." The creature stared at Raffi. "I don't . . ."

"He's right." Raffi came and took the Coronet reverently from its seven fingers. "This isn't something only one of us can do. It's for all of us. And we can't reach the Sekoi. You can."

The Great Hoard

Reaching up, he put the frail gold circlet on its head.

The creature's eyes narrowed. For a moment only the snow fell, silent.

Then it said, "Raffi, I can see! I can see all the way to the stars!"

28

*Flain was the last to enter the door. He
looked back and it is said he wept for
the Finished Lands. "I see now," he said,
"that we are the world. Deep in our souls
lies the evil one."*

*Tamar came back for him. "Not unless
we wish it," he said.*

Book of the Seven Moons

IT WAS A CIRCLE OF GOLD and they were all inside it.

For a second Raffi knew the vast arena with its treasure was a huge replica of the Coronet; as the Sekoi argued up to its people in the Tongue, he felt the consciousness of the gathered tribes slowly and reluctantly enter it, the sharp anger of the Karamax like seven stabs of pain.

"What's happening?" Carys muttered. She still had the bow aimed at Solon, but he sat still, as if listening.

"They're joining in." Raffi glanced down at the still form that was Kest. "The power of this will be incredible."

"Like Tasceron?"

"Better." It was building already, a hum and murmur of energy that abruptly assaulted all his senses; left him blind and deaf until he knew that he was one and many, that the Coronet and the arena were tiny concentric circles far below him, and that this icy silent nothingness was space. It was black, an emptiness, darker than Maar. It stretched into infinity and all their minds together could never reach to the end of it.

Until, like a miracle, something existed.

It was a globe, pale and smooth, bright with reflected light. The curve of its edge was perfect and breathtaking. It hung from nothing. He turned, looking for the others.

They were all around him; the Coronet of Moons, Agramon a little way out of line; impatiently he gave it the slightest nudge back into place and it drifted like a bubble. Raffi smiled.

"*It's a sophisticated form of neural integrator*," someone was saying, but he ignored that, knowing that the circle was smooth again, that he wore it like a Coronet, that the mingled lights were in proportion.

Now for the weather. But where was Anara?

The Great Hoard

Then he knew that he was the planet. He was the world. In his body were all the aches and agonies, the vortexes and storms; he searched for them and flexed them out, absorbed.

"*Not Solon!*" the wind protested, but he hushed it, smoothing the roaring waves on the beach. Someone was bleeding on the gold moons; he wiped them clean and put them back in the sky. Snow stopped falling into his eyes. Carefully he opened his hands and let the small flowers stir, the trees blossom in the cracks of his palms.

"*Bring me a present!*" a small voice wailed. So he rolled up winter and threw it away, unfolded a field of gold and spread it like an eiderdown over hills and valleys and mountains. "*What a joke,*" Marco laughed, from underneath.

And a thin, brown-haired man opened a door in a vortex and stepped out, the storm shriveling behind him. "The others will deal with the rest," he said. "But you I need to warn. Give me your hand."

Raffi held it out. Kest took it and turned it over. "Look at this."

They were deep scars. Seven wounds in his own skin,

seven deep pits. He stared at them in horror, at the poison seeping from them; then he gasped with pain, his hand still clutching Kest's.

But the voice that spoke had a reptilian hiss. And it said:

"Raffi."

His eyes snapped open.

The arena was cold and empty. A faint breeze drifted over the heaps of gold. On one of them the Margrave sprawled, looking at him.

Its long, jackal-snout was a profile of horror, the moons casting bizarre shadows of its sharp-eared head and dark coat.

"What do you want?" Raffi whispered.

It gave a lipless smile. "You know what. And I was so close! Solon even held the device in his hands, and it was your fault that I lost it. But then, I have learned about so many other things! The Crow! Since my dark creature met Galen at Halenden I have known my ancient enemy was back. Sarres, of course. And the Great Hoard. I'll send a whole Watchforce to collect this. And now, I have you."

The Great Hoard

Raffi shook his head. Terror was creeping over him like an eclipse. "No. No you don't."

The Margrave laughed, a harsh rattle. "You and I are linked, Raffi. Ever since you came into my room in your vision you have intrigued me. I learned more about you in those few seconds than you think. We are linked. I have rarely talked with a human soul like this since Kest came to plead with me in my prison."

Its small eyes stared at him, the lids swiveling like a lizard's. "I'm going to find you, Raffi. Bring you back to my room. I know you have hidden qualities; your master doesn't value you enough. I'm sure you've often thought that." Its tongue flickered in a sly grin.

"I need a companion and I have chosen you. You will be my apprentice."

Raffi gazed at it in utter horror.

Beside him suddenly Carys came back, then Galen, stepping moodily out of the dark. On the ramparts the Sekoi tribes blurred out of nothingness and in the sky the moons came on like Maker-lights.

The Sekoi, tall and astonished, reached up for the Coronet and took it off, staring at the gold ring in amazement.

Only Solon sat on the pile of gold.

The Margrave left him. They almost saw it go, saw the absence creep into his eyes, saw him become in an instant a heartbroken, devastated old man, unable to look at Marco, unable to look at any of them, huddled up and sobbing.

Carys turned away. It was Galen who went and crouched before him.

"Leave me!" the old man moaned, hiding his face. "You see what I've done!" His eyes caught the knife handle; Galen moved in front of it

"It's over," he whispered. "The evil is gone from you."

Solon looked up, his eyes wide. "I couldn't keep it out! Dear God, I couldn't!" His cry was an agony of remorse; he looked imploringly around at them all, rocking with pain. "Three years, Galen. That was how long. Every day, every hour they tormented me. Never letting me sleep or think." He gripped his hands together. "You can't imagine how it was. On and on, lights and questions. I couldn't eat. I forgot who I was. I forgot how to pray."

"I know." Galen held him firmly. "It's over now. We'll get you to Sarres."

The Great Hoard

"And then he came! He explained how I could help him. He spoke softly, and I let him into my mind, Galen, I let him! I couldn't bear it anymore, the filth, the pain, the darkness. I couldn't even bear the smell of that room. I wanted him. He made me strong. He gave me power. In the end I was begging him to come."

There was a bitter silence. Then Galen said harshly, "None of us can judge you until we have been through such a hell. But Mardoc's Ring. All the things you told us. Were they true?"

"True. But he forced me to tell him. He found the ring and wore it, mocking me. I have betrayed everything I loved! And yet I would still do anything rather than go back to that cell!" Solon clutched his head in despair. Galen watched. When he asked the next question Raffi knew it had been an effort.

"And the child? The one you cured?"

"He did it." The old man looked up, seeing Galen's eyes close in despair. "He's clever, much too clever for us. It's over. He has all of us now."

"Galen!" Carys's voice was sharp. "Look at this."

Above them, in the air, a door was forming. They stared

up at it, Raffi gripping the beads at his neck in silent awe.

A narrow door, with a silver staircase that unfolded silently and smoothly like a ripple of light to the Sekoi's feet, so that the creature jumped back in alarm.

They waited. No one came down. The door stayed shut.

Around the arena the Sekoi tribes watched in fascination. "Are the Makers here?" Carys asked. She felt a sudden panic, as if she wasn't ready; she stared at the door as if Flain would open it and walk down. It sparked a sudden memory. "I forgot! He told me something else! He said, 'Tell the keeper I'll see him soon.'"

"It's the portal." Galen's gaunt face was shadowed, his eyes dark with joy. "Remember? The console said the Coronet could make an emergency portal. This is it! A door to the world of the Makers!"

He gripped the handrail and for a moment Raffi thought he would race up and fling the door wide, the desire so keen in him that Raffi could feel it.

But he didn't. He jumped down, hauled Solon to his feet, and put his scarred hands roughly on the rail. "You go," he said.

The Great Hoard

"Me?" The Archkeeper was aghast. "I betrayed them! I've done evil, welcomed evil. I can't face them!"

"We all have to face them." Galen stepped back. "No one is turned away. This is your chance to make up for your weakness, Solon! Do it for Marco, for all of us. Get them to come! Tell them how much we need them, that the Unfinished Lands will still spread, that men's faith has grown cold."

Solon glanced at the others.

"No!" Carys crossed to Galen and faced him angrily. "It should be you! He's weak, you said so yourself."

"Weakness can hide strength."

"Don't give me that rubbish!" She glared up at him, but he wouldn't look at her. "He betrayed us, Galen! You must hate him for that!"

Then he did look. "Not him. And the Crow has work still to do here." For a moment the hardness of his eyes softened. "Don't tempt me, Carys," he whispered.

Shoving her aside he said to Solon, "Go quickly."

The Archkeeper wiped his face. He took a small bronze ring off his finger and dropped it into Galen's hand. "Choose a better Archkeeper," he whispered, and turned and climbed the stairs as if each one was an effort of will. When he reached the top, the door slid open.

And for a second they glimpsed another world; a pale sky, green fields, a warm breeze that lifted Solon's hair as he walked fearfully into it, fluttering his coat in a scent of alien leaves, lighting his face so that in the instant before he vanished he seemed young, laughed, held his hands out to someone, and Galen had taken two steps after him before the door closed and the light was gone and the staircase dissolved into moon-shimmer.

It was very quiet in the arena. The snow had stopped. In the black sky the moons hung, each in its appointed place. "I wish Marco could have seen that," Carys muttered.

She bent and picked up a leaf that lay there and handed it to Galen. It was long and narrow, some sort of willow, Raffi thought. And alien.

"It seems to me," the Sekoi purred, looking up at Agramon, "that I moved her."

"It was me." Carys threw the bow down.

"Me," Raffi said.

The Great Hoard

"All of us." The Sekoi stared at the Coronet. "How can I tell you how it felt? Like the joining of many stories, all at once." It looked up, yellow eyes sharp. "The Karamax are coming down."

"Will they let us go?" Carys asked.

It shrugged, laying the Coronet reverently between Kest's hands. "It may be they will. Things have changed now." Suddenly remembering, it took off its money belt and emptied a stream of coins onto the heap. They tinkled and rolled. "Though I fear all this must be moved to a more secret place." It looked at Carys sidelong. "I have to say, Carys, that I have been wrong. I am sorry."

She nodded. "So you should be. Mind you, at one point I suspected you." She grinned at Raffi, who was pale and still. The Sekoi turned. "And you, Galen, don't let the darkness fill your soul. Despite the deaths, we have achieved our aim."

The Relic Master came forward. He put both hands down and gripped Kest's coffin, and Raffi felt a sudden sickening jolt of terror.

"Galen!" he muttered.

The keeper's face was harsh and set. "I swear," he said,

"by Kest and Flain and all the Makers. By all the Moons. By all the Books of the Order . . ."

"Galen, don't!"

". . . By all that I've ever believed—I swear the Crow will hunt the Margrave down into the deepest pit of hell for this."

His fists clenched. "And when I find him there, I'll kill him. Because of what he did to Solon. And for Marco."

He turned, his hair glossy as a bird's wing. "I swear it, Raffi. I will never forgive this."

Raffi felt as if all his nightmares were drowning him. He looked at Carys.

She shrugged and picked up her bow.

"Be careful, Galen," she said quietly. "I somehow think that may be just what he wants."

The story concludes in

RELIC MASTER

Book 4: THE MARGRAVE

I think you should confide this fear to your master, the tree said gently.

Raffi gave a sour laugh. "No point."

He is, I admit, difficult to approach. A small sparkbird, brilliantly red, fluttered among the branches; the tree rustled thoughtfully over Raffi's head. *If he was one of my kind, he would be holly. Or dark firethorn that grows in the chasm of Zeail. Such a one is Galen.*

Raffi nodded. He lay on his back in the dappled green light, eyes closed against the sun. The tree was a birch; young, and very curious.

Tell me where it takes you, this Deep Journey.

Excerpt from THE MARGRAVE

"It's a vision." Raffi sat up and gazed out hopelessly into the depths of the warm spring woodland. "It happens in your mind. The Litany says there are different stages—the Cosmic Tree, the Plain of Hunger."

Hunger is a sensation?

"Emptiness. No food."

Indeed. The tree sounded fascinated. *Our roots are always storing. Rootless creatures, it seems to me, are most vulnerable. The Makers were wise, but sometimes we feel you were something of a failed experiment.*

"And then," Raffi said, half to himself, "comes something called the Barrier of Pain."

The tree was silent. Finally it whispered, *You fear that.*

He nodded. "And the last thing even more. To be a keeper every scholar must pass through utter darkness into something the books won't even describe. They call it the Crucible of Fire."

Fire! The birch shuddered down to its very roots, every leaf quivering. The sparkbird flew out with a cheep of alarm. *Fire is the worst of enemies! The Watch burned the forest of Harenak, every leaf, every sapling. Who could fail to mourn so many deaths?*

Excerpt from THE MARGRAVE

"Raffi!"

Galen had woken in a black temper. He came out of the shelter, still looking tired, and snapped, "Any news?"

"Nothing."

"As soon as there is, let me know." The keeper turned, tugging his black hair loose from the knot of string. "And stop wasting your time. Read! Flain knows you need to."

Raffi picked the book up without glancing at it. "He's a nightmare," he muttered, "since Marco died."

The tree was silent.

Galen limped between the birches to the stream. He waded in, scooping the cold water up to drink, splashing it over his face. For weeks he had been working on the sense-lines, driving himself nonstop. Already they had a chain of lines between a few known keepers and through re-awakened channels of tree-minds and earth-filaments that reached to Tasceron itself; in fact last night, after days of effort, Galen had spoken with Shean, the keeper of the Pyramid in the Wounded City. It had been a triumph. But it had worn him out.

Looking down on him, Raffi thought of the night of Marco's death, of Galen's terrible oath, that he would seek out the Margrave. That he would kill the Margrave.

"That's why he's so desperate to set the sense-grid up. And to get me through the Journey. He thinks he won't come back alive."

Now, the tree said gently, *you are really afraid.*

Raffi jumped up, brushing pollen from his clothes. Already it was back, that sickening terror he could never lose for long. He felt the tree's consciousness spiraling into him, intrigued.

Do you really believe, it whispered, curious, *that this Margrave is hunting especially for you?*

"I can't talk anymore." Raffi turned abruptly, blocking its voice out. Sickness was already surging in him, a choking stress, blurring the tree-words to a crackle of leaves. He started to stumble through to the stream, then swung around for the book, feeling the sweat on his back chill as he bent, dizziness making his vision spin. He gasped and leaned on the tree.

Raffi, it said urgently, its voice bursting through his panic. *Someone comes!*

Bewildered, he felt for the sense-lines. They were intact.

Excerpt from THE MARGRAVE

"Galen!" His voice was a whisper, a croak, but the keeper was already racing up; a firm hand grabbed him. "The Watch?"

"Can't be. Can't feel anything." Weak, he crouched on the tree roots. Galen spun around, facing the footsteps.

It was the Sekoi.

Wiping his clammy mouth and streaming eyes, Raffi staggered up and tried to focus, but the creature was close to them before he could see it properly. Then he stared. The Sekoi was worn and ragged. Dried blood clogged its fur from a half-healed wound under one ear. Its yellow eyes were glazed with weariness.

Galen grabbed its thin shoulders. "For God's sake, did they ambush you? Have they got the Coronet?"

Exhausted, the creature collapsed onto the leafy bank. For a moment it seemed too worn out to speak. Then it whispered, "The Coronet is safe in Sarres. We were on our way back when we ran into the Watch."

"Thank God," Galen breathed, but the Sekoi seemed not to hear. Over his shoulder it glanced at Raffi. "They've got Carys," it said hopelessly.

RELIC MASTER

From *New York Times* bestselling author of *Incarceron* and *Sapphique*

CATHERINE FISHER

Welcome to the world of Anara.

FOUR gripping installments.

FOUR consecutive months.

ONE epic adventure.

THE DARK CITY

THE LOST HEIRESS

THE HIDDEN CORONET

THE MARGRAVE

Collect all four.

RELICMASTERSERIES.COM